GAEL

Judith Mok

GAEL

TELEGRAM

British Library Cataloguing-in-Publication Data
A catalogue record for this book is available from the British Library

ISBN 1-84659-006-X
EAN 9-781846-590061

This edition published 2006 by Telegram Books

TELEGRAM
26 Westbourne Grove
London W2 5RH
www.telegrambooks.com

In memory of my parents,
Maurits and Riemke Mok

Her violin. On the first day she had it with her on Torca Point, a small cliff at the end of the park. She'd walked down with their son, his small, dry hand in hers, her violin on her back. They stared down at the deep sea, breathing in the unfamiliar smells of gorse and veronica, not speaking at all, listening to the wind and watching it play with the water against the rocks. The pull of it. Down, down. And then they came out of the water – the boy counted them – six dolphins swimming against the warm current. It was October, the month they always came up towards Dublin Bay, but neither of them knew that. They imagined, both of them sharing the same childish hope, that these dolphins were messengers. It was going to be good, their life over here. The child's face was full of joy as they watched the kaleidoscopic swirls in the sea below. She took her violin from its case, telling the boy that she was going to make them dance for them, for him. I could see and hear them so clearly from my hiding place. They had no idea I was there, their phantom father and husband. I was witness to the miracle they were about to create. I could see the sky stretching over the blues and greens, shrouding the Sugarloaf Mountain, keeping very still above the spot where the dolphins would appear once again.

She started to play the Brahms violin concerto. Out in the open it sounded like a folk tune. The boy clung to her coat, waiting anxiously for the dolphins' reappearance. And two of them did return. They turned and bowed to each other in the air. They splashed the water high with their tails, silently singing to the tune. Mother and son saw the droplets sparkle in the bleak sunlight. She played for a good while – until the creatures swam up close to the rocks and then, just as suddenly, departed, leaving them staring into the empty water. Then she put her violin away and kissed Samuel. They were laughing and talking about Ireland. How wonderful this welcome was.

I followed them back to their new home.

1

'So what's it going to be? Murder or suicide?'

Women like this were what he had hoped to find on his little trip back to Dublin where, in his earlier lecturing days, he'd enjoyed the splendid squalor of the Trinity College rooms. If he were to feed his *nostalgie de la boue,* a pub performance by this creature would be a good start.

He ordered a drink.

'If you listen to me, your head will be spinning for weeks.'

She had kept her eyes lowered but now, as she repeated the same question, she flashed them at her public. Just long enough for him to recognize her.

'What's it going to be? Murder or suicide?'

He suddenly realized that he had returned to Dublin not for a bit of local colour, but to find her. She, the one who was going to tell a tale of love and woe and play her fiddle on a makeshift stage.

'My name is not Molly,' she admitted.

She was not Irish, but a Jew from a cold Nordic country.

'Do you like sentimental stuff or the real thing?'

Her voice was hoarse.

He peered around in the shadows of the bar to see if anybody was paying attention but no one seemed interested. She loomed in the background, a frivolous piece of amusement. Though that's not how it felt to him. To him it was story and revelation time.

She stood very still, her arms glued to her thin body. A bad spotlight brought out the dye in her ragged hair.

'You have to think of me as a ghost, but one that's alive. An entertaining one, I hope?

By 'ghost' I mean that my body and voice, and certainly the life I'm supposed to have now is mere fiction. I am a memory come alive.

Okay, here's how I met my Irishman. There was this thing he said to me when I first saw him. I had so many words, he said. Had I kissed the Blarney Stone, he asked. The *what*? A stone from his country. I thought they only kissed stones in Mecca, or the big black one I'd seen in Jerusalem.

My coat was dripping with blood. Some stranger had bled on me during a fight in a café. The stone man followed me into the Mediterranean night.

Inside he had already managed to tell me that I wasn't beautiful but strangely attractive. As though I'd never heard that one before. Where is the beauty? In the touching or the looking – or the fact that his knees were getting weak and he wanted so obviously to be inside me. We wandered through the night, nameless. We sat eating fish at five in the morning, watching people go to work. I had a husband at home. Our home. In another city. In another country.

And I had my violin.

It was waiting for me in my cold apartment with the tiled floors and the solitary gas heater. It was snowing that night when I decided to leave my violin and accompany my friend Gertrud to the train station.

My flatmate came with us, cursing the fucking climate, while my friend Gertrud quietly longed to be back home. She had booked a comfortable bed on a high-tech passenger train, with one of those pointy, shining engines that can nearly take you space travelling. But all we found was one desolate latrine car on the track. It was big, bulky and dark, with a huge spout sticking out ready to release its dirt. We teased Gertrud, saying that that was her train and she nearly believed us, but then she smelled the stale urine and realised her trip was off.

A bunch of scruffy men followed us around the immense station as we searched for a telephone to call Gertrud's partner to tell him she would not be home that night. But none of the phones worked. The men were yelling at us, and my Scottish friend shivered. We were frightened.

We left the station and crossed broad boulevards trying to find a café or hotel that might have a phone that worked. It kept on snowing.

That night was my first time in a real brothel. Our Scottish friend had re-discovered his courage and had to take us there: it was a place to use the phone, he joked, smiling mischievously. While Gertrud made a nervous call to her beloved I settled into a red velvet chair and observed the comings and goings of clients. The door opened and closed to let in the snowy air and silent men who made their way upstairs. I ordered a taxi, sent Gertrud back to my flat and decided to follow my flatmate to a downtown café, where I met the Irishman.

It couldn't have been a coincidence that I had just started reading *Ulysses*. It was a rare wartime German edition that my father had given me. Like Proust, Joyce was a must-read in my family. I hadn't yet made the connection between Dublin and the island of Ireland, let alone with this nameless night wanderer who seemed drawn to me despite my deplorable lack of beauty.

He was wildly beautiful. Strong legs. I liked his legs as much as his intelligent conversation. All through the night he talked colours and people. I talked about parts of my life, music. Nothing was real.

We kissed like teenagers on my doorstep for about an hour, and then I went upstairs and hid in tired confusion in my bed. His lips had that taste. Hot, red blood. Throbbing. I touched my mouth in the darkness of my room, felt my lips against my fingers.

Back then I was a soloist leading the orchestra. Playing with the locals, earning a reasonable penny, which I brought home to my husband every second week. I kept mostly to myself in that city by the warm sea. It was just that night that had been different. It was like a wave, a wild tune in me that I felt sometimes. I had to wander into other worlds, troubled ones preferably. And then I could play better and get solo work, and people would applaud my music and me.

The orchestra was not for me. My husband was happy enough with the experience it gave me, but he saw me as a solo player. He didn't care about the money. There was plenty of that where he came from.

During my Mediterranean absences I never heard much from him. That must have been the reason. Why I kissed the Irishman, I mean.

He dropped in a few weeks later. My mother had come over to stay with me. While I made tea and fussed with cups, they started a lively conversation about art, which was the thing my mother most liked to talk about. I kept getting up from my seat. I wanted to move my body right in front of him. He fixed his shiny amber eyes on me. I didn't get an intelligent word in edgeways that night, just stared at his ragged clothes and tried to restrain myself from stroking his hair. He gave my mother a small catalogue of his paintings that he'd brought with him. Did he create a bond between them to seduce me? I doubt it. He told me he would contact me and show me the real life of the city. He was bragging about his wild acquaintances. His stories were lost on my mother and me. All she thought was that his paintings were impressive and, well, everybody can be young and a show-off.

So let him roam the wilds of this city on his own.

But I didn't. The grind of the train wheels home and back affected me; repeated words turned me into a romantic, turned into wishing, turned into me picking up the phone and inviting him out.

We were not lovers at that time, though it was spring with hot gushes of wind and the irresistible smell of flowering jasmine made us weak with craving ... We'd sit in cafés and restaurants by the sea, behind steamed-up windows if the day turned cold. He held my hand, told me about the mothers in Ireland who go out and steal meat for their family in the supermarkets. Only on Saturday. Only once a week did they have meat on the table. It was perfectly acceptable to steal if you had no money. He came from a neighbourhood where stealing was the norm. I weakly protested that I'd never been to such a place. But he was away with Marx, the underclasses and condoms you could only buy under the counter of a record shop.

All the usual Marxist bullshit I'd heard before. As for condoms, as yet I didn't understand that condoms and other methods of contraception were not available for everyone in Ireland. We kissed a lot, let our fingers explore the shapes of our bodies, and he came to listen to my 'fiddle playing', as he started to call it. Late at night we'd eat and talk. I never thought about the fact that I always paid the bill. He knew all the places with great views, great ceilings, or great food. And so I paid. I paid to hear him talk about Dublin, where he'd been taught by Jesuit priests. Where people ate grey food out of newspapers and got drunk on brown beer. Where you puked and discussed your hangover and its degree in vivid detail. Every time he told a story I was showered in 'fucks' and 'fuckings', while I sat in my designer French outfits dreaming up the other person in him – the one who'd tell me his mother could hardly write but knew how to milk cows and talk to them in the first harsh hours of the morning. His granny would sing soothing songs while waiting at the crossing for the train to pass, so that her animals wouldn't get upset. He traced little drawings on the paper tablecloth of animals running towards us. But his father was a city man, accustomed to the monotonous rhythm of factory work. He came home to a bossy mother and eleven older brothers and sisters. There was always enough to eat. They kept pigs in the yard, where the toilets were. People chained to primal needs, with no words of comfort but those the parish priest had to give.

Occasionally a quiet young man would join us and nod his appreciation of his friend's accurate description of their homeland.

I couldn't stay sitting beside this friend for long because he smelled so bad. Neither of them had any regard for cleanliness. A full bath on Saturday, and one spin around, that did the trick. Clean enough.

I'd had plenty of lovers. Everything was always clean in my well-organized young years. Especially sex. My father always claimed that sex was good if you were in love. While we did the dishes my mother would teach me about safe sex. So I developed a shining, erotic universe. Whenever I loved and lusted after a male I expected earth-shattering orgasms. This Irishman who talked his way into my affections and was worthy of great sex put the scrubbing brush between us. As I did my husband.

He took me to his studio a few days before my orchestral contract finished. I saw that he was talented, really talented. I had learned from my father, who was a great painter, to look at art. As children, we'd been forced to visit countless museums and galleries, to read books on the subject. I'd even modestly attempted to draw. I thought I had no virginal response to art, but his work made my response virginal again. Tough, harsh colours, furious lines. To me it was obvious that nobody could ignore it. At the time he had sold a couple of paintings to a New York gallery, but had to earn his living with drawing lessons. Lessons to women named Carmen and Carmel, to the fiery Dolores del Fuego and other dark-haired beauties who would drive him off to their homes on the back of their scooters.

Often in the early afternoon, after we had sated our sexual frustration with a variety of tortillas, I would be left standing alone on the pavement waving at a yellow scooter with my as yet platonic lover perched on the back, hands held firmly around some other woman's waist.

2

Gael the painter has met Maria. Gael should have been a priest. He is devoted to Maria who speaks a foreign language and he has lost all beliefs along the long road from Bethlehem to here. Here they are, beside the hot mirror of the Mediterranean sea reflecting her naked, muscular body. There was a hard sun in the sky to shine on her, to catch the colour of her hair for him. So he could go with the taste of her lips on his and find some red clay and wet earth, and rub it on the painting. For blue he took the generous sky without even asking, and dressed her in it. His icon had lips and eyes to talk to and a body in a shrine. A priest in the Roman Catholic Church with his mother Maria minding him. Already he followed the sound of her boots and ate their shadow, keeping their imprint for holiness. Maria came from Botticelli and Rosetti, to show him how she really looked. Gael the painter used rough sand on his brushes. 'Believe in Maria' had been pounded painfully on the palm of Gael the schoolboy's hand ... But he had washed it off with the grey of rain and the white of wind, and at home had watered her further down with his mummy's bleach over their very own print of Maria. Once she had lost her face he started looking for her, the real one. The Jewish girl that would leave herself for him, for he was the only priest in her church. The priest that could recreate her a thousand times and love them all. Maria came from Cranach and Holbein, she came from the North, her skin ever so cool against the hot air that lost them. A stern face against a sensual background, a burning horizon. No animals could breathe yet. He still held all of them contained in him. But he would show them to her when she minded him, her priest. Roman Catholic still because he is chaste in her church and only loves her in his painting. Because he can show his life in her image. What he saw as a five-year-old altar boy nearly crumbling under the weight of her statue. He was carrying her around the church outside, slippery stones under his shiny, polished shoes, black shoes, black stones wet, and black trousers on the priest in front of him, but when he looked up in the dark of the evening he could not see her under her saintly skirt, for she had folded her legs and the darkness in between them in stone. He painted the wet statue and tasted the salt of her secret in his mouth. He was ten years old when he first received her cold kisses and now he marbles her lips and her skin, so thin the veins, yet so visible they could bleed when you look at them.

Maria stands at a street corner, her cheeks touched by the weather, alive with a hidden smile, cloaked in a woollen cape that hides her teenage body, holding the case of a fiddle in her arms, singing to it as if it were him she wanted to tell that she already knew him then, in the concrete Bethlehem where her parents were pork butchers and he was the little Catholic boy who had just lost his faith to her, a little Jewish girl. He never talked to her and now he paints the corner of that street, the lack of light and contour, the damaged paint on the woodwork, the rain dripping off the rust on to the street where her footsteps stand.

As long as he believes in Maria they will come to him, Rubens and Raphael, and offer him the full fruit, the basket of shades, and hand out colours early in the morning. She stands beside him while he works on her and talks about his slaves. He tells her they are her slaves; Carmen and Lulu, his scooter girls, have to draw her, only her, until their fingers hurt.

Here is the city. It has its buildings for humans, for music and dance, food in the streets, knives with real bloodstains on the floor in bars, and the soft, wounded skin of the coat that belongs to Maria when the city meets her and he is in it.

Maria who talks his language with a silver tone while he starts his painting of her walking with the stars rigid in the night sky above her. Never will he mention these. He will unscrew them and turn them into demons that will tease Maria into love, tease her into duty, the duty to mind him, the priest in her church populated with demons. They are silent and watchful, in awe of her talking, in fear of her bow and her fiddle, and the unpaintable thing called music.

3

I went back home, back to my husband, only to dream of Gael. Between concert halls and rewarding melodies, foreign countries, holiday beaches and books, food and friends, talking and writing, visions, sex and stupor, he remained. So when the offer of a new two-month contract with the orchestra came up, I went back to the warm city by the sea.

He did not know I was coming back. We had kept our feelings to ourselves, and only a letter and a postcard in casual handwriting made it to my home during half a year's absence. Much and nothing was said in those messages. I picked up the phone once to call him, but when I spoke to him all I could do was listen to the background noises of partying and Mediterranean fun. So I cut our conversation short. And I never wrote to him, not even to tell him I was coming back.

I made the journey with a middle-aged antique dealer who had let me his apartment in the warm city. He needed to go there as well, to visit his mother, he said, and he might as well give me a lift.

We drove for twelve hours to arrive in the late evening. A huge wine celebration was taking place. While he drove me to his apartment, dragons and grotesque medieval figures feasted around our creeping car. We had opened the windows and the air blew a hot breath of alcohol in our faces.

I was drowning, drunk with the knowledge that I had come back to this place where the Irishman lived, in ignorance of my presence. Tomorrow I would ring his doorbell and climb six flights of stairs to his apartment, just as I had rehearsed it in the last six months of dreaming. We arrived at my apartment. The antique dealer, who had hardly said a word throughout the entire journey, brought my leather bags full of clothes upstairs. He showed me around the place. It was big, full of Art Deco furniture, and it smelled. What did he keep in the cupboards? I asked jokingly. He didn't smile but announced that tonight he was going to share the only bed in the place with me. It was too late for him to go to his mother. I was still holding a case with toiletries in my hand and was close to the door. Without a second thought I went for it, ran downstairs and found myself on a broad avenue full of tipsy people. The city was partying. I bumped into tables full of wine bottles and baskets overflowing with grapes. Young men talked and whispered, hissed and whistled close to my face. It was two o'clock in the morning; I had no choice but to ring the doorbell of my future lover.

It was noon the next day when I woke up in his arms. We had talked so much in the past that that meeting was silent. A ritual burning of everything said, a measuring of our flesh. The unexpected leap of him into me, his wolf-like sexuality. Here was an animal I hadn't encountered before. My body felt flooded with orgasms; under a sheet of flame. He circled my ankles with his hands, tenderly wondering how they could be so narrow. Teasing my fingers into decadence while his admirable member started swelling yet again. The combination of such lust and love started closing in on me like a cage. I already knew, back then, that without this I would hurt myself banging away at its walls.

We collected my luggage and I secretly moved into Gael's room decorated with revolutionary posters. My husband was not the type to phone very often, so I rang him and told him about the obnoxious antique dealer and how I now shared a flat with a couple of artists that I'd previously met. He sounded vaguely uninterested, but happy I had a place to stay, no doubt happy he was alone with his work. Or maybe just quietly happy for me.

There was not much room to analyse how I felt about my husband at that time. Somehow I was wearing the elegant cover of what I imagined to be French grace, but I didn't explore the material it was made of. It was so much easier that way.

Whenever our bed was not a playing field, it was because of work. Music, painting and lessons were a useful blur that resulted in money for food, which was consumed in bed. I juggled around a lot with my credit cards to procure us luxuries in the form of underwear, exciting hotel rooms on the coast if we didn't make it home, and material for him. For he was painting hard between six and ten in the mornings.

I played with the orchestra and instead of working on Bach's solo Partitas I scratched away at songs about girls rolling over in clover, and taties that were out in the springtime. Or bits of broken melodies that he'd hum for me in which I could hear Arabian undertones, so close, so close to some sad Yiddish tunes.

Did he know? I sat naked on his bed on an overcast Sunday and made my violin sing for him. Sombre Sunday was the title of the song. A suicide song. Well, in Budapest mostly, where people were sombre anyway. He listened and laughed away the tears in his eyes while he started warming his hands between my legs.

He loved potatoes. With what? Butter. Did I know there had been a potato famine in Ireland and that millions of people had perished? So now he had taken the hunger of those masses upon himself and ate only potatoes. Okay, butter as well. We were standing at the kitchen sink in the late afternoon, trying to figure out a meal that would satisfy both our foreign palettes. I forced some red wine down his throat. Little Jesus in velvet trousers. What? The wine like a precious hostia. He folded a potato between two slices of bread. There: a chip butty. Great delicacy. Love it. The sheet he was wearing had slipped and his strong white limbs were all too visible. A delicacy. And here's my dish. There was only juicy me. Me...

I was there in golden boots and a very short skirt. Lost to reason before breakfast. Ignoring opportunities to audition for solo work. Spending a lifetime of love in a couple of months. Just that and I would go home again.

But there and then I lived with him. That I had a husband was a mere notion that helped me pay for our martinis and Sunday lunches in the park. We never discussed the moral aspect of our liaison. Morals were scarce on the ground in that city, which grew sunnier by the day. I lived with him in my music and in the paintings he made of me. It was understood that I would leave at some stage soon. I made him take showers with me in the morning. He made me stand in cafés and bars; if there was only one seat available, it would be his. That surprised me more than it bothered me. I took him to concerts of classical music, and he howled with laughter the first time he saw a balding quartet of oldish men working away at their instruments in an immense, badly lit hall. He didn't hear the effortless melodies they produced; he saw only their raw, rather ugly appearance. It made me shrink from him, judge and immediately forgive.

We would stand outside the concert hall with a whole night of love ahead of us. He held my hand and talked me into a wild session of clubbing so we could forget the ugly four. He said he would marry me if I hadn't been married already. No use explaining that in my Europe people got divorced. I was married and he was too much. Too much on the rough side of a life I could not live. But never enough of the dents that his deep voice left when he spoke to me in the dark, never enough of his hands on a canvas showing me where his life was, never enough of his body and mine floating attached or unattached through the same sensual seas. Never enough of him hiding in a silence where he could hear only me. The shells of his small ears tasting salty, pink where the curls touched them or where I did. Never enough of losing control. Not that I said these things. I just cultivated them so I could leave without the unbearable pain of separation.

We went to the Palacio, one of his favourite nightclubs. I took to wild dancing, and he took to wild drinking with his old friends Carmen en Merce and the other dark-haired beauties that seemed to be close to him. I had no friends there. I had him. The Irishman.

4

She talks and plays, and acts out the story of a life. Loth sits in the dark, talking back in silent images. Mute memories of his life with her before the island became a shadow on the map of her brain.

They had big tarnished copper pots. Emilie, their housemaid, loved to polish them and stare at her distorted reflection.

His wife had just walked in, barefoot as usual. Small feet, high arches, her nails dark. Loth would buy endless amounts of shoes – Jourdan, Saint Laurent – to dress them and make them even more desirable. But there they were, flattened out on the black and white kitchen tiles, innocent-looking. Their cook's rabbit came to sniff at them.

She always sneaked downstairs in the afternoon to chat with the cook. She wanted to be *au fait* with the menus and the wines that needed to be ordered. She loved to watch the dog and cat asleep together in the basket. But above all she loved the light in the afternoon. Somehow it reminded her of Pieter de Hoogh, who always kept a door or window open in his paintings, to let in that peculiar light, signifying life, hope, promise. She would rattle on about the light, not knowing that her husband spied on her through a little window in the *entresol*, a cupid's eye that had probably been put there to check if work was being done properly in the kitchen.

Loth remembered one perfect afternoon in October. It was the time they call *entre chien et loup*. The light in the kitchen was at its best, tinted by the warm autumn. The kitchen was alive with food. They were having some writers or maybe a minister for dinner. She was talking about food, he was sure. He couldn't hear her. Her bra strap bit into her arm. The house pets moved around silently. Her feet tapped a heartbeat on the floor.

He suddenly saw how in a few decades she would be a total eccentric. He could even imagine her living under a bridge. But there, in the embrace of that afternoon, he was sure she was happy.

On their first evening out between Sèvres Babylone and Chatelet she had already made it clear to him that he couldn't compete with the trio that they were going to hear perform. He couldn't think music. He could explain it all right, she said. That was her opinion after she had been to one of his lectures on music at the Sorbonne.

She still amused him, bemused him. She had made fun of his suggestion to go to the zoo on a first date. To watch animals fuck behind bars? Then how could he possibly enjoy the Beaux Arts trio? Laughter changed the colour of her eyes; love struck him instantaneously.

She laughed as they walked towards the Theatre de la Ville. She didn't mind that the wind was turning the ends of her beautiful evening dress into ridiculously flapping tongues. She was right; all through the concert his love of music was tempered by his love for the straps around her ankles. He was simply sitting there to enjoy her.

After their *souper* he suggested that they should become lovers. 'Maybe for a month,' he suggested modestly, 'if you'll have me that long.' 'Are you for rent?' was her answer. She didn't have a lover just then. A Swedish acrobat had juggled with her heart, had made it bounce and then break. This man was into sugar-coating her. The idea was attractive.

And there was something about him that was new for her: that you could actually formally ask somebody to become your lover. Her 'yes' made him lie down beside her on her theatrical bed, his eyes carefully stroking her. Keeping his movements small and delicately sensual. Looking at her quietly, looking at her all the time.

He was allowed to drive her to her Nordic country in his Jaguar. They shared a stupid weakness for cars. They had to be old, sleek cars.

Being her lover entitled him to visit her home. They drove along grey skies on perfectly drawn motorways. Being in the car gave him the sensation that they could travel through time together, that they were in a timeless vacuum. She was sitting beside him, her legs on the dashboard, talking, gossiping, watching the landscape that wouldn't last longer then a few minutes until they reached the flatlands. He had never liked the flatlands.

She told him about her father. His refusal to look at the past. The faces of his murdered family members that appeared in his paintings, hidden in a mist of abstract colours. Sometimes he didn't speak for days, because he was concentrating on his work and that took him back into the suffocating reality of death, of multiple deaths, of an eternity of death. She seemed to describe him in big lines against that never-ending horizon that they drove towards.

Her parents lived in a house on the canal, with tall, narrow rooms and ornate ceilings. Her father's hair shone like a silver crown against the light in the marble entrance hall. He embraced his daughter and kissed her warmly. He made small talk: did they have a good trip, was the weather bearable, had they eaten? He took their coats and peered through the glass door to make sure their car wasn't parked too near the water.

His French was fluent and heavily accented. As was her mother's. She was silver-haired, too. Slight figure, light voice as if she was about to laugh. A smooth face without a wrinkle; the suffering of the war had left no trace. She came from a wealthy background and had become destitute after the Germans had taken over her family properties and bank accounts. When she'd met her husband she'd been as poor as he was. An eighteenth-century silver spoon was all she had left from her parental home. She showed Loth the spoon. It was small and elegantly decorated, just like herself. A slim, silver object.

The house was warm and pleasantly lit. Her father suggested drinks. With filled glasses in their hands they went around looking at his paintings and the works of many of his famous friends. He was a small, stooped man who moved quite quickly and asked pointed questions, jumping rapidly from one subject to the next. He clearly had an encyclopedic knowledge of a wide range of subjects. But he seemed modest enough, and kept apologizing and joking about himself and all his talking, all the time gazing at Loth kindly, inquisitively. That his daughter had brought a lover home was nothing special; all her acquaintances were welcome in their house, welcome to share their food, to share her bed, if that was her wish. But she had expressed an intention towards this Frenchman and so he needed to be tested. Gently.

Loth had been warned that these people had no time for sentiment. They loved their children and fed that love from the roots up, every day of their lives. Wandering out into the world was part of their growing-up; their education was going to make them stronger, enable them to adapt to any culture. No matter what the circumstances were, or the people they would mix with, they would have to learn to understand. Understand absolutely why people would want to murder them, extinguish them.

Yes, Loth thought, they were rather impressive. Pity they had no real money. This clever painter had made very little out of his name and talent.

Although it was Friday night, no prayers were heard and an old *menorah* stood candleless on top of a bookshelf. He sat beside her, quietly taking in the modern furniture and the healthy food. He watched her hands move as she described a concert, people, a painting she had seen. As they talked the family grew more excited, shouting almost, although he had no idea why they were getting so worked up.

The wine was good and loosened him up so he could show some brio in the subjects he at least knew something about. He was amazed at the almost physical pleasure the family took in conversation. He loved the cold analytic feeling he had when analysing a musical score, and the equally cold admiration he felt for certain performers. But the feeling was not sensual, as it seemed to be for them.

He admired her feet in bed that night. And her drawings,

realizing for the first time that she did have another talent. She had told him before she liked to draw.

Now she laughed about her mother's cooking. Servants had looked after her, and then she had just gone hungry. And the furniture, *oh la la*. She teased him in a manner he found very amusing. It pleased Loth that she seemed to be making some allowances for him. His elegance obviously attracted her. Her thoughts. He wanted them. To spin a web through his brain so that maybe he could see into the movement of her feelings.

Breakfast could not be spoiled was his first thought when he woke up entangled in her long curls.

Her father greeted him very formally that morning. The table was laid with a white linen cloth and napkins, fresh bread and coffee. Or would he rather have tea? Her mother was friendly but aloof. Both old people were immaculately dressed. Their daughter was still in bed. Waiting for her mother to bring up her food on a tray. The cats would follow. He remarked on the cats, who sat devotedly by her father's chair. Yes, the old man admitted, these were miraculous animals.

Loth stared at the fat tabbies, sceptical of their powers, while eating his toast.

Had they plans for the weekend? Would he like to visit the studio? Her mother asked all the questions while her father stared at an indefinite spot on the table, shaking his head from time to time. The old woman chatted away as if she were at an English tea party. She was nervous, she kept rubbing her hands together so that he noticed the big liver spots on them. She had to be much older then he'd originally thought. She babbled on about his car and how she'd learned to drive in a Bentley as a young girl. But just as she'd reached the perfect level of elegant small talk, they took a dive into the hard facts of life.

Nothing changed in her facial expression behind the slow clouds of her cigarette smoke as she mentioned German cars and how some brands had also provided gas for the camps. Had he seen the books upstairs in his bedroom? How could he have missed them? There was some interesting material about that period, maybe he would like to read some of it, or take the books back with him to Paris? He said he had some knowledge of the period. Some knowledge, the old man imitated him, and again shook his head, yes, yes, very good, he murmured. Was he interested in the great German painter Max Beckman, and did he realize that he had lived in this country during that period? He'd kept fascinating diaries, in German of course, but naturally Loth read German, any musicologist would read German, would they not? As a matter of fact Loth did read German.

All this at breakfast. He asked her parents if he could have a go at the piano. Of course, they would be only too happy to hear him play.

The scores lay scattered on the piano. Loth chose some pieces and began to play. Her father stood behind him, hopping from one foot to the other, now humming and then swaying as if in a religious trance. When Loth stopped, her father laid a hand on his shoulder and told him that his sister had been a good pianist, that these were her scores. He looked at the biblical name on the sheet music and bit back an overwhelming emotion.

They hadn't noticed her standing in the room in a tiny night slip, with her violin hanging loosely from her hand. Her mother had already provided her with a coffee, which she slurped in great haste. He had not yet accompanied her. Today was beginning to look like an all-round skills in art and life exam. She stroked his hair, nibbled his neck and then came the hissing: come on, be good. While he deciphered a piano version of the Brahms violin concerto she had turned her slip into a stage dress and performed. He could hear her structure, her line, he imagined he could even hear some feeling. Within himself.

Once it was over there was a silence in which they all moved towards the more practical things of daily life. It seemed to Loth that the others had to make an effort to find them.

Now Loth was sitting in their old Citroen, squashed in the back between her and her student brother who had just turned up. While they drove along they sang songs in whatever language came to them. Her mother had a raw voice and shook her silver curls as if she was an old gypsy. Perhaps she was. It made him decide to be careful. Careful in his judgement of these people who, after all, he did not know, and were now singing in their ridiculous old car. She was dressed in a long, red coat with furry edges and a velvet *flambard*, and seemed a bit out of place to him. Had their few months together turned her into this flamboyant being? She was well dressed when he'd met her. Her mother was elegant. Her parents had laughed about her designer outfit; she was such a snob, they said. How could soft fur against a perfect cheek, the clinging of cashmere against a sensual curve, be snobbish? It was the way to forget that they were sitting here in an uncomfortable vehicle.

She could be modelled into a wine connoisseur, she could be a hostess. The raw material was there. She even managed to move her high-heeled boots from one canal-side cobblestone to the next with grace. Her family had provided her with some riches, at least. The rest was up to him. He would marry her without being overprotective. She would have to work hard at her art. Everybody could be a good professor or a reasonable pianist like him, but her talent was an asset. An asset that could be pleasant when in the company of friends. She could travel and live her life freely. How good it would be to go to one of the great theatres and hear her excel with a famous orchestra.

Her father was very consistent in his self-imposed duty to educate Loth about the city. Meanwhile he never stopped pointing out the light, the way the sun was setting, and the clouds. Jubilation. Sensations altogether not to be missed. Loth felt tired by their persistence in pointing to and recreating the world. If Loth saw perfection in a building or bubbling up in the bloody sky he wanted to be the master of his own discovery. Your daughter is a delight, he said to the old father. She is, and the phantom of it, was his reply.

Loth was touched when her father asked him if he wanted to wash his hands before dinner. He did not know then that it was like a ritual that remained of a religious past. He had noticed that the same sort of thing seemed to happen with the bread; it had to be broken with two hands. Never cut. When they had visited a museum the whole family seemed to be totally *au fait* with the biblical subjects in the paintings. They were comfortable with lamenting old men with names such as Job or Jeremiah, the melancholy subjects of Rembrandt's art. Or Susanna's pale young body and a sneaky old David lusting after it.

There were to be guests for dinner. Her student brother had taken over the kitchen and reproduced some of his cook's favourite dishes. Loth had discussed them with him on their way back in the Citroen. His sister laughed and teased him about it. Medicine man was going to cook. Their parents laughed too, because, yes, he was a great cook but food was not so important. They had done without it for a while. Both grew silent at the same time. Her mother was driving. She was obviously the experienced one. Her husband pointed out some windmills along the road, quietly.

He had been curious to know who was going to be there for dinner that night. Some painter and writer, arty-farty friends, she had answered in the same teasing tone she had used with her brother. She fumbled with his ear and babbled about food. She still had a lot to learn, Loth thought. She had not met his cook yet, with her extensive cookbook library and her biblical wine list. Not much food in the Old Testament as far as he knew. They, of course, took great pleasure in contradicting him. For the rest of the journey they enjoyed their new game: naming food from the Bible. It was a good game, and fun. They thanked him for it.

But now his hands were clean. Clean enough, he hoped, for the famous guests who arrived dressed in vivid velvets and large hats. Loud greetings and embraces followed. He shook some firm hands and looked into faces he had regularly seen on television screens or in catalogues. They were friendly faces with the same inquisitive eyes as his lover's father. He couldn't help noticing their formidable noses. Two men and a woman.

Her brother served his dishes with panache. They were greeted with enthusiasm but quickly forgotten. The conversation easily outshone the food. Daniel de Barrios had appeared as the groom in Rembrandt's *Jewish Bride* since the painting had been cleaned. Nobody had known it was him, the Spanish poet who fled to Tobago and then to the North. He had been painted by the great master, who later changed the painting and uncovered his once-covered head.

De Barrios? The large colourful woman writer screamed. They were all screaming. At the top of their voices they discussed de Barrios' adoration of the False Messiah and his Turkish followers.

He noticed her, his mistress, antique earrings dangling from her soft lobes, a woolly gold dress, slightly overdressed as seemed to be the norm here, eating with intense pleasure. She listened and interfered with dry comments. The Messiah's Nordic followers, taking their ritual bath in the frozen canal? *Meshuggas!*

How strangely modern the cutlery and porcelain were, the square-cut crystal and the candleholders.

Would he convert to Islam or choose death by decapitation? The satisfied faces looked at him inquisitively, demanding an answer.

'I am a man,' he had started. They nodded, that much was clear. 'So, it is of course an easier choice for me than for a woman.' No answer, heads shaking. 'Well, considering the cuisine of the Islamic Sultan...'– a slight disgust appeared on their faces – 'the doctrine of Islam is worth studying before one dies.' They started to laugh; was he a Jew, never to give a straight answer? They abandoned the seventeenth century to discuss present times. All seemed to be members of some foundation that took care of human rights. Even his lover lost some of her levity in the light of humanity and its more murderous aspects.

'Some champagne?' He had brought it from his own Paris cellars. They drank and took the bottle under their arms to climb the stairs to their host's studio. The moment had come to inspect new work.

5

Please drive carefully, her mother had said when she kissed him on both cheeks. So he drove his lover back along the same easy roads, back to Paris. She had to tell him everything about her mother if she was not going to drive at all.

'Forget everything you see, start with a clean slate, and just listen. My mother.' Which part of her mother did he wish to discover? All sides, all parts, every adventure, every lover. You have four hours to fill with your mother's life. Until they reached Paris the roads were only there to be covered in stories, histories.

My mother, Anna Henriques.

They had houses, they had servants, dogs, cats and a large wealthy family. When Anna was very small they had a carriage and stables for the horses. Her nanny, who she shared with her five brothers and sisters, used to steal her mother's silk stockings and then beg the children to put them back. This was a routine that went on for a couple of years. Stealing was just a game, so the children thought. Her mother never noticed. Or so Anna believed. She was allowed to try on her mother's hats and shoes and silk taffeta petticoats and dance with her sisters in front of the mirror singing her mummy's favourite song: 'whatever you do, be sure to marry a Jew'. Her mother was a well-known beauty in the capital and she loved to socialize. As soon as a child was out of nappies she would take him or her shopping and drink hot cocoa in one of the richly decorated Jugendstil cafés. And one day Anna realized that her mother was different. It was in just such a beautiful café. It rained small lights from the chandeliers and it was nice and warm with the winter dark outside on the tall windows. She was deeply involved in a piece of *sachertorte* and did not pay any attention to her mother's richly dressed and perfumed friends. They were rather loud and the next thing was her mother towering above her – she could count the buttons on her bodice. She was standing on the café table amongst the porcelain and the cakes, talking about women's rights. Shaking the feathers and plumes on her hat at some people, asking for votes for women and equality for the poor. Anna noticed that she was not wearing a silk petticoat but a simple white lace one. And she felt proud of her.

That night Anna went to her parents' bedroom and looked at the books on her mother's bedside table. There were French novels and books on German philosophy. They were bound in leather and the pages were wafer-thin when she flipped through them. Silky like her underwear. She must have been about nine years old, old enough to understand that these were foreign languages. From places they had visited, such as Deauville in France and Vienna to visit Herr Mahler. In France her mother would laugh and drink with people who came from Russia like her ancestors, and her father, who had a beautiful tenor voice, would sing after dinner, just for fun. Her father was always away in countries like China or America. And when he returned he never came alone. The guests would stay for months sometimes. He would bring home lots of presents and china or precious linen. Her father did not read much. He liked music and football.

Once, in Vienna, they had to be very quiet in a big building and sit still for hours while her parent's friend waved his arms in front of a lot of people with musical instruments. When it was over Herr Mahler came home with them.

On a bad day, when she came home from school, she found that somebody had shot her dog. With her brothers she buried him and then went to sit in the dog's basket in the kitchen. To cheer her up her mother gave her a book of poems. Her first. It gave her comfort that there seemed to be something outside the language she knew and used every day; another language lived. She started reading obsessively through her mother's library. A lot of poems were learned by heart and spoken out loud on long walks or when she was bored in the company of friends. They started calling her eccentric.

She grew up, and there was the girl's gymnasium and the balls and parties and Madame Rausch for her evening gowns and Hirsch for her hats. The parties where the young Louis Armstrong would play with his band – all the way from America – for the jeunesse dorée, and she would flirt with her admirers. The boys in tuxedos. Everybody smoked, of course. Everybody made love, of course. A young baron got her pregnant, but he was an empty-headed beau so far as she was concerned. Her parents suggested marriage. But there was to be no wedding, just a visit to Switzerland to have an abortion.

She continued to read (plays, poetry), until she went to see her father in his study to ask him if she could join the theatre.

He was a mild man, totally devoid of religious feelings, but it so happened that he was glancing at the *Torah* that day and having a fit of morality. He was happy with his quiet afternoon in his warm house and here was his learned, beautiful daughter who wanted to go on stage. Had she lost her mind? He picked up the telephone and asked to be connected with England. She was to enter society over there and, it was hoped, meet a companion for life.

She went for a walk with her mother along the empty beach. She was docile, she would go, the theatre could wait.

On their way back from the beach they walked through the village. Boys shouted the usual insults at them.

England suited her for a while. Being the well-bred yet glamorously rebellious one. Poking fun at little ladies in hideous hats during endless tea parties and picnics. There is a photograph of her in a short fur coat, radiant, having a picnic with her friends in the hilly fields. And there is a man sitting in the photograph, at a bit of a distance. It was their chauffeur. He also had to have lunch. Having the chauffeur in the photograph was a solecism, of course. But Anna had insisted.

She became engaged to a well-behaved young man. He liked to read and was planning to turn the rest of their lives together into a comfortable journey. But she had to wear trousers and sing with jazzmen after hours. They wrote songs for her that we still hear. She perfected her English, fine-tuned her accent. The young man was too virginal to marry.

There were a few years back at home, auditioning for the theatre after all, moving away from her safe society into bohemian circles. Pictures of her with a cigarette. Her slim body dressed in low-waisted silks, long necklaces. Attractive artists laughing at her side. Always laughing. Until her father was shot in Berlin on a business trip. He had been drinking with friends in a nightclub and had started singing a Yiddish version of the Song of Songs. Somebody in a brown shirt got up and shot him.

Her mother died six months later, of grief it was said. They were the lucky ones.

Let's skip those years. Just to relate that her brothers were killed and her one remaining sister went insane.

After that she was moved to a sanatorium in Switzerland. Too ill to live outside its walls, but well enough to read and start translating literature, and acquire a wide knowledge of modern art.

When she was back on her own two feet and moving around her home city as elegantly as possible in her rags, she took to visiting galleries with those of her friends who were left. They were still wealthy. She had lost everything, her parents' wealth confiscated by the Nazis, and she survived in her friends' mansions, working as a translator.

She left with the painter who became her husband, at the opening of his first postwar exhibition.

Impressed by his talent, she recognized him as the young man who had helped his father out in a deli shop she used to visit with some friends after dances, after hours. While they sipped champagne she would joke with the old man, who turned out to be strangely erudite for a shopkeeper. She had hardly looked at the thin young man beside him.

That was her as well: opinions about shopkeepers, shoes with wooden heels, people eating without napkins, wearing clothes that were not made to last, not made out of natural materials.

Her children were brought up with strict codes of etiquette in their modest house. But it was impressed upon them with so much charm that the silks and Egyptian linens were acquired naturally, as naturally as the way their mother liked to mix several languages. Her stories about the diamonds that she swapped for food sounded like fairytales. They could not imagine the woman in the kitchen, singing and making a mess of the cooking, wearing a ball gown and a diamond necklace.

Some of her friends were like that, though. Ladies in pearls who seemed to admire the work of her sadly not very well-to-do husband.

She took the children to her friends' houses and taught them to feel comfortable around them. Money was never mentioned, but bitterly missed. They met with royalty and Russian princes, ate *piroshkis*, stuffed cabbage sandwiches, and cried and partied with refugees from the Revolution. Much kissing and sobbing, loud talk and arguments were the lines along which their lives were mapped out. She was seldom sad. Her past was void, but at a mature age her future had been filled with two children and a husband who fascinated her. She never knew how to handle a household. Her family had shopped in the best places. She tried to do the same. The house overflowed with paintings and books. And then there would be the gaps, which could last a few months, when there was nothing left to live on. But she did not complain, though her mouth would tighten, her smile seem less generous.

Her children were deprived of nothing: they had food, music lessons, clothes, and were driven around in the oldest of two CVs, enduring their parents' endless songs. It was she who suffered deprivations at times. She loved to give, to present people with what they most wanted. These people were always articulate, of course. A foreign language had to be spoken perfectly. German writers were her favourite. She shared her husband's views on Germany: a divided country with a lot to offer.

Their sorrow was personal and seldom mentioned. When her children wanted to know where their grandparents, aunts or uncles were, she told them the truth: that they had all died.

There was no room for death around her house. Active learning, music, joy. A stream of energy that made her regularly collapse into old war illnesses. Her husband had no patience with illness, and her children quarrelled with the housekeeper, coming to complain at her bedside, at home or in hospital. She always recovered, and turned into a healthy *grande dame*.

That was the older woman she was now. The woman he would certainly meet again. They had reached Paris.

When he parked the car she turned to him. Did he understand that she *did* question her parent's life and possible lack of pragmatism? That she realised she had picked up the superficial joys of an acquired taste for material things? They lived with a pain they couldn't share with her. She had arrived when the smashed pieces of their existence had been glued together to begin again. She could only try to help them reach the finishing line.

6

Before I left he wanted me to go to Ireland with him. Just for the week, he said. So I lied to my husband about a music trip, and he believed me because it suited him that way. I didn't waste much thought on it. He wasn't going anywhere.

For some reason I flew to Dublin one day after my lover. He would be waiting for me at the airport. I looked down at the threatening waves and the threatening mountains before a cloud devoured us and I saw no more of my future.

The carpet at the airport was brownish in colour, with millions of dots, and it smelled. Just like the carpet at the airport in England. I had been told that there was nothing remotely similar between the two countries. I dragged my heavy bag along.

He was not there in the hall as promised. I decided to go for a coffee.

I asked for a cappuccino, and the waitress served me black water in a mug and planted a jug of cream beside it. Here you are now, she said. It lasted me long enough for him to appear. His face was swollen and he had a plaster over his nose. He handed me a rose wrapped in tinfoil. When he kissed me, he tasted of stale alcohol. Before I could say anything a long story was unfurling from his hungry mouth (I could smell his hangover stomach) about the night he'd spent with his friends and how he'd had a fight with a cupboard. Hence the nose. It was broken. He took a bit of the plaster off and showed it to me; it looked like a Greek ruin.

He wanted me to buy him some breakfast. That would give him time to tell me about his adventures and how he had planned my stay in his homeland. While he worked his way through a plate full of greasy substances, he told me about the cottage he had rented for us in the countryside. His countryside, where his ancestors came from, princes and kings all, the original pirates and thieves of Ireland carrying his name, he said proudly, while he used his sleeve to wipe the last of the greasy food from his lips.

His friend had invited us to stay over for the night. I shook hands with a bearded person whom I couldn't understand, though he seemed very friendly. I said thank you. I ate his food, and threw up afterwards. I asked if I could take a shower or a bath. Ah no, he said, that's where he kept the beer. That night I felt like I was making love in a prison cell.

I also felt I had come home.

We took a train through the green countryside, passing flowers, rocks, cows, until we had to change at a place called Limerick Junction. I had been listening to his lengthy explanations of the places we saw from the window. He kept holding my hand so that it grew warm, and with it my entire body. But now we were standing on a platform in a bare nowhere. It started to snow.

There was no shelter. It was here that I started my first battle with the winds.

For an hour-and-a-half at least I tried to hide in his coat, behind his back, but whenever I moved my face met the elements. I had to talk to them, convince them that I was here for a reason. I peered at the grim backdrop to the station to seek distraction from my cold feet. My feelings were paralysed.

A train pulled in to platform one. It reminded me of a train I had last seen twenty years ago in France. My father had pointed it out to me then as a curiosity. It had been the last of its kind. Here it lived on in a time of its own.

Snow covered everything, so I couldn't admire his ancestral land on the taxi-drive to our rented cottage.

It was a low-ceilinged house with a living room and a bedroom. It was bitingly cold. We stood and waited for the landlord to arrive. My lover said he would make a fire. I was familiar with making fires for fun but not in a house. He asked me to deal with the landlord while he heated up the house. I paid the rent for a week to a man in a woolly hat.

We had a fire and a snow-white view, but no food. The slide to the village took us half an hour. More men in caps, big chunks of meat on hooks in the butcher's window, a shop that sold baked beans and white bread. And butter. A search for vegetables would have been like digging for gold in the mountains of Holland. My lover's diet and demands seemed to have changed within a few days. We were going to feast for a week on sausages and baked beans. And worse: my warm underwear did not appeal to him. It was pink, with frills in the wrong places, and it was very hard to remove.

After we had dined with our coats on and watched the flames die out, our only source of warmth was bed. So we went to bed early and I tried not to remember the other countries and my other life. He told me stories about his ancestors chasing people who were chasing sheep. He drew them for me on a small drawing pad. And as they started to live I started to laugh at their dark faces and their blunt weapons until I felt our bodies come alive again. Nothing was real apart from his skin and his hands that loved me. When I felt weightless with exhaustion I kissed his broken nose and fell asleep. Soon dreams moved in that took me back to reality.

I woke up because somebody had stuck a mask on my face. It felt stiff and I could hardly breathe. The cold was so intense that it felt frozen; when I opened my mouth a big gust of steam came out. I hid under the thin blankets until the smell of coffee and fried eggs reached me. I felt my way around the bed to see if I could find a jumper and a pair of trousers and quickly got dressed.

He was standing in the half-light of winter with his coat on. Later he would make a fire; we'd run out of turf. I liked the novelty of burning turf. A pleasant feeling came over me; this was not going to last. I was a tourist enjoying a preparatory trip for a survival camp on Nova Zembla. The name appealed to me, so maybe I was unconsciously planning to take a vacation over there. I rambled on to my darling, ignoring the faint voice in my head telling me to call my husband. We pushed our food through our chattering teeth and decided to go for a walk to thaw our feet.

There was no telephone in the house. I couldn't call.

We held on to each other, children in a silenced landscape, writing a kind of truth with each footprint in the virginal snow. We reached the village, only to hear the news that there would be no traffic for the coming days, and a food shortage. I discovered a telephone and dialled my husband's number.

He sounded slightly amused that I should be snowed in. I didn't need to bother to call him again in the coming days. He felt I was safe in a cottage built of snow. 'Never knew you had primitive aspirations, darling.' His laughter sounded loud under our high ceiling, the ceilings of my home.

Meanwhile my lover showed no concern; there was a car-racing competition going on in the village. Men in knitted caps – some pink – drove as fast as they could backwards through the main and only street of the village. The snow caused the tattered cars to slip and slide like toy cars at a fair. Grannies and children giggled along the road. I went in search of fuel and food.

We spent the whole week talking about his work and his plans. How he wanted to avoid living his parents' life. In their time they had assessed their needs, reduced them to the basics and struggled with stupefying work to pay for them. Church events were cheerful occasions: a good funeral meant a large amount of drink. And drink meant a warm mist of oblivion for a couple of hours. His bleak images made me feel even colder. I liked listening to him talk about his childhood. How he had a horse in front of his house in the middle of the city. A horse he could talk to and later show his first drawings to. The heavy silence of his parents whenever he showed them a drawing. They had a couple of images of The Lord on their walls. So he drew The Lord for them. His mother hoped there might be money for him in it. She prayed for it. She knitted and she prayed. A lot. She couldn't really read or write. They watched the telly. That's what you call it. The telly brought the world to them. But they switched the world off and only watched soaps.

There was the ritual measuring of the willies with his friends, and how his was the biggest. Of course. He showed it to me again. And we made use of it. Again. He made a portrait of me. My drawing of him did not work out, so I kept tuning the cold strings of my violin. I played. I played along the lines of his thin stories and heard a clearer tone coming to me, and a different structure.

I also learned to practise making loud farts in bed. His idea of fun. The beans certainly improved my abilities. We never went out much. Only once did we venture along a stretch of road to visit a pub. We were the only splash of colour in the uniform landscape.

The pub was nearly empty, apart from a few middle-aged whiskey drinkers. For some reason I had brought along my violin. We drank and exchanged words until they asked me to play a tune. I produced a simple tune by Bach. Their loud clapping was pleasant; even here, having played for these people made me thaw out, thaw back to myself.

A man who had introduced himself as the chief of police told me he knew a girl called Hadassah Roth back in Glasgow, where he'd worked for a while. She was a great fiddler, that girl. I mentioned that she must have been Jewish with a name like that, and I was just about to say that Jews tend to make good fiddlers when he interrupted me. 'Jewish? Jaysus. You mean to say that the old guy Hitler didn't manage to get rid of them all?' It had started to snow again when we struggled back to our dwelling. He was holding my hand. All was white in the bleakest of worlds. White can be so cold once it has lost its innocence.

He said he had reserved a room in a hotel on the River Liffey back in Dublin, but when we got there this didn't seem to be the case. No matter, there was plenty of space, so I dug out a card and got us the room. I was going to meet his parents the following day.

It was grey. Everything was grey: sky, trees, streets, houses, cars, the view, people, all grey. He left me in the Auld Dubliner, a large pub with carmine red sofas. It smelled of decades of smoke and stale beer. I tried to breathe through my mouth – and kept my gloves on while I sipped mineral water.

He was going to come back in ten minutes. Just needed some time to warn his parents about my imminent arrival. Me – the girl in the photograph they had seen – his girl, he said –ah no, they said, that's a lady. Me – the lady on the stained couch. It took only an hour for me to disintegrate. It took him two hours to return, to order me to follow him.

At the door she waved water at me. Holy water, for she had heard I was not a Christian. His mother, a small, fat woman took my coat. I noticed that her mouth went dry when she spoke to me. We talked about the snow, something she knew I was familiar with. I stood in the airless hallway that was filled with the smoke of fries, noticing the statues of her holy family. I kept my hat and gloves with me on our way to the kitchen where more holiness greeted me. A plastic heart beating in a plastic representation of the Son of G. I sat down and waited for my cup of tea. Meanwhile my lover discussed the neighbours and the deceased with his mummy. He called her Ma. I tried to imagine my mother's facial expression if I had called her so. It cheered me up. The thought of my mother – that I could go and see her soon.

While we had our tea she told me they'd had a Jewman in her village. He was a pork butcher. The joke was lost on her. I began to enjoy myself, except for the cold. Could I ask for my coat back? Let's go and meet the Da, she said, before I had a chance to mention my coat.

The father was sitting in a low-ceilinged room with his legs stretched out in front of him, a cigarette stuck to the corner of his mouth, a beer on the floor beside him. The television was on loud. Clearly he was not going to get up from his comfy chair. The room was decorated in a variety of flowery patterns strewn over the walls, the curtains and the sofa. There was just about room for all that. We sat on the sofa, the silent mother and son with his foreign lover and the relaxed father in his TV chair. We drank our tea. The father spoke. He liked Spain he said. Did I want to know why? I could barely understand him, but I nodded politely. Cheap drink. His smile was triumphant. Surely I did not expect such an answer? I did not. But now he wanted to know if I liked Spain and, if I did, the reason why. I mentioned the landscape, the language, the rich cultural heritage. I decided to be ambivalent in my praise. I was a snob. I was a snob because a line of a Spanish poem that I loved came to me and I did not care for cheap drink.

Why not talk about their country? But we seemed to have visited a place they called 'the bog' and they did not want to talk about it. I thought it had a different name.

The visit was a short one. When we were back on the asphalt he explained to me that people from Dublin always laughed about the countryside and called it 'the bog'.

I left. I left again. I tore myself away from his tales that kept me on my toes, his crudeness that peppered my sensualities, from the blatant knowledge that I had been stripped of a comfortable way of interpreting myself and my music. His mere presence hit me harder than ever before. At the core a feeling that I refused to recognise as love. So I went my way.

The way of my tunes. Let me give you one.

7

My husband asked me, very politely, if I could tell my Irish friend not to ring at two in the morning every single night. He did not mind the bunches of flowers or stained envelopes that arrived on our doorstep. But his sleep was sacred. He did hope that the man was a decent painter. Think of the disgrace, my dear, if he turns out to be mediocre. But his problem was soon solved; a small portrait of me was sent to us. It was very blatantly dedicated to me. My husband praised the work as technically excellent, as well as interesting in shape and colour. I sat at the breakfast table hugging the painting. He suggested bringing 'my friend' over. It could turn out quite well, to have a talented ruffian around for dinner now and then. An artist with a story to tell; enough to last one course during dinner at least. I felt I was looking at my husband through a telescope. Since when had he managed to develop such a stable position in the universe? And at exactly what distance were we now existing from each other? He was going to inquire about an apartment for my painter friend. That silenced me for some time.

I was thinning into the prescribed shape of a true *Parisienne*. To me it seemed that if I were lighter there would be less of me, less of his imprints in my flesh. I could feel them everywhere. I became neurotically addicted to water, to wash him out. Water down my lover's touch to a flow I could integrate into my life

Women at an old sports club, of which I had become a respected member, saw me swimming for hours in the pool and then steam up in the ancient Turkish baths and finally sprawl in an old armchair with a notepad trying to figure things out on paper.

The afternoons were fanatical studying hours, my fingers shredded, the blotch in my neck from the violin turning to a purple bruise. Evenings were either the voices of guests or music at my concerts, or living with the presence of his absence.

I slowed my backstroke one morning only to discover that there were Stars of David all around the ceiling of the pool. I had never regularly visited synagogues but I did recognize one if I happened to be in one. I climbed out of the water and, dripping, went to see the person in charge of the club. Not enough Jews around to keep the place going so the health club had bought the building, was her laconic answer to my question. The Chief Rabbi's room was the Turkish bath. Naked women relaxed in the room where wise men had once tried to understand the world according to their doctrines.

Painting nails and hairdos had taken over from the commentaries on the Kabbalah. I sat in an old armchair, speechless with surprise, and had a good look around. It suddenly seemed to me that all these white and very naked bodies were being oiled and perfumed for the ultimate sacrifice of their souls. As soon as they had painted a mouth on, they were only allowed to talk shop, such as hair, weight and designer outfits.

No one was allowed to mention the smelly old men who had conferred here, in this same space, to talk about the miracles of life and death. The pool might have been a ritual bath, a *mikvah*. That idea appealed to me. So I cleansed myself of the stains of an adulterous love.

I sat in my chair, stark naked, until the pattern of the cover was indented in my skin, until I started laughing at it all.

We had agreed to meet for lunch at Fouquet's. The restaurant where James Joyce used to go with his entire family and hand over enormous tips to the headwaiter. I had to be thinking of the Irish connection, of course. I kept humming cheerful tunes, walking all the way up the Avenue Foch, all the way down the Champs-Elysées. Looking at the trees, smelling the spring in the breeze, waving at a man in a car: forget about sex, forget about it and don't turn it into that emotion that you do not want to hear about, just forget about the sex.

I had paraded a second lace skin in front of my husband the night before. He had sat behind his desk, his legs slightly apart, flawless fold in his casual trousers gazing at my underwear, my high heels. A tinge of sadness in his eyes. I took advantage of that and cajoled him into my consoling him. We had a short struggle with sex, as short as the word itself. He sighed into the pillows and admitted to admiring my outfit. It just did not turn him on. My body, after all, was an empty orbit.

Walk. Forget that he is naked behind you, and worse, his long fingers in you, on you. His hands stroking your skin. That magnetic field is drawing them closer to a firm grip. Male. I had that long, dull poem to be recited along every walk I took.

He told me over oysters and lobster, his manicured hand resting peacefully on the damask tablecloth, that he had found a flat for my protégé.

His answer to my raised eyebrows was that he had checked my credit card accounts; the young artist did not come cheap. The gesture was cold. My answer was a photograph of the Irishman kissing me passionately, which I put down beside his plate.

In that case, he thought, I should take another trip over there, just to say goodbye and put an end to the whole business.

He took my arm and we strolled to a travel agency.

I spoke to him on the phone. No need to collect me. He was just about to forget all about me, about the time I came to see him. So he said.

If things were like that I might as well throw my ticket away. But no, I was what he wanted and I was just going over there to show him he was not, ever, ever going to get me. That time he picked me up and took me straight to his bed in a filthy cold room.

His canvasses stood around doing most of the talking for him. I explained the facts. We were not to meet again. He laughed and said it was fine, fine with him.

We had two days of loving to do. Could we sleep somewhere else, I wondered, after I struggled for a while to find my clothes amidst the ruins of his belongings. Ah sure, we could go out and phone a friend who lived in his grandfather's house. A beautiful big redbrick. I was marched along a gloomy street. Drizzle hung around us. I didn't notice the dull facades well enough until we reached our roof for the night. We entered the sombre hall. It was late. The friend showed us to his grandfather's bedroom. The old man was in the country, so we could use his bed. I undressed my freezing body and pulled back the bedclothes. On the sheet was a long, dry shredded piece of skin. I suggested the old man must have been a reptile. And I could not rest in a reptile's nest. We went downstairs and called our host. Not a muscle in his face moved when he heard our complaint. Granddad was not a great one for changing the sheets, but there should be some clean ones in the bottom drawer. They were his Granddad's wedding present. We found them and enjoyed the fifty-year-old dust in our dreams.

For breakfast we met a girl who did not introduce herself. To avoid the sausages I listened to her talk. She was all praise for the house, she was from the countryside and they had a toilet outside in the yard. I couldn't believe my ears. The girl kept on talking. She was away with the animals on the farm and the fire they had to keep going. There was a sickening smell of hot, dead fat.

I fled outside. A group of born-again Christians were singing in the garden next door.

It was tuneless and messy; their singing pulled at my fragile nerves. Back in the kitchen the girl was now wiping the remains of her breakfast from her face with the back of her hand. At least she had stopped talking.

He took me to a show, and once the lights went out quickly found his way under my large silk skirt. At the back of the theatre it was cosy and warm. I'd forgotten to put on my knickers that morning.

We met girls from his past on a lot of grim street corners. They all shook their fingers at me in warning. Not that they wouldn't meet up with him again themselves, but just the occasional thing, you know. I did know. Could I at least see the shadow of one of his true crimes before leaving, I asked him? He laughed. He was still laughing when I turned around to wave.

The relief I felt was because I was leaving that country, not him. Not him.

But his time was up.

8

She laughed. She kept laughing up and down the monumental stairs, through the large corridors, inside the warm rooms of his house. It was the first time she'd seen it and he'd already asked her to marry him. They had met in the Métro where she stood playing, rehearsing for a music competition and earning some cash on the side. They had become lovers in her tiny apartment. She was not to know about his place and his people until he knew that she was right. After a few months he knew: she didn't care for money. The day he bought her a necklace and asked her to marry him was a funny day for her. She had never considered getting married. Men were for love, yes, but only music was for life. She kept her laughter going for half an hour at least until she met his butler.

He had insisted on wearing his white jacket the first time his boss's fiancée came for lunch. She shook hands with the pale, middle-aged man and asked him if he lived in the house. Yes Mademoiselle, with my panther. She wanted to know all about the panther immediately, very pleased with the man's eccentricity. It turned out that his panther was just a name for his girlfriend. It made her stroke his arm; having such a weird servant was good indeed.

They met them all. His old seamstress who insisted on telling her that Monsieur always ate with a napkin, even when he was alone. She, too, was dressed in her best black dress and white lace collar. When they reached the kitchen he gave up and went on his way to the library. She could become familiar on her own with the cook and her help, Amelie. There would be much to talk about. Or so he thought.

But she just sat very quietly at the big scrubbed deal table and listened and watched them preparing the food for her lunch with him later on. The cat had settled on her lap; she felt its soft, round head under her hand. Cook talked and handled the knives like a circus artist. Chopping vegetables, shaping them into coloured mosaics, using a fine long blade to cut the bloody red meat. Raw meat, she said, she loved raw meat. Cook smiled and immediately wanted to know what kind of wine she would have with it.

The answer caused her to blanch. Master would crucify her if she served that. Cook laughed again and handed her a wine guide.

There were long shelves of cookery books and wine books at the back of the kitchen. With the wine book in front of her she started to study, while Amelie, the kitchen help, sang wordless songs interrupted by manic chopping sounds in the scullery.

The butler wore gloves during lunch and tiptoed around the huge table to serve them. She kept trying to enter into conversation with him and he kept hinting at her not to. She drank far too much wine. Strands of hair came loose, she wanted to sit on her fiancé's lap. She told him stories, wildly gesticulating with her hands. She turned into a Jewess from the Dreyfus period, dressed in her white lace dress, bought somewhere in an obscure second-hand shop, no doubt. It suited her classical features and it suited the neo-gothic decorations of his dining room, but it didn't suit him to have her with him as a romantic heroine. She had to calm down a bit.

His miserly parents were mentioned in unpleasant tales in order to detoxicate her.

Their traditional anti-Semitism was something she had to be aware of; it was the norm amongst the French upper classes. He was telling her this to prepare her for their visit to his parents. Another matter was her clothes. She had taste and grace and he loved her, but she needed grooming.

That afternoon she lost her voice in the carpeted showrooms of prominent designers. Transparent young women moved about elegantly in the casual clothes she was supposed to wear. Their dolls' eyes never met hers. Her fiancé sat with legs crossed, sipping foam off his cappuccino. Darling, I like you as a *gamine*, darling stay out of the reds, darling a heel that style is very *rive gauche*, that's good. So they were not from the other Bank. She realized the importance of the *philosophie* behind her looks. It was the *Nouveau Philosophie* crowd she was supposed to mix with, play for, get paid by. A few hours of fashion and big spending had made her. She was now officially his fiancée.

Now she had to enter the crowd of his *normaliens* school friends and seduce them. Young men and women who spoke subjunctive French and used the formal *vous* to address each other. Who knew which knife to use for which cheese and, more importantly, the perfect angle at which to cut it. Their competitive interest lay in who invited the most important *savant* or politician for dinner. A ground rule was never to discuss a television programme. As they strolled past brightly-lit shops, he explained to her how his friends had all gone to the same Grande Ecole.

She wanted to buy roasted chestnuts in the street. Eat in the street? He watched her eat from a paper cone and wiped the crumbs off her coat, muttering that she ate like a pig. Pigs love chestnuts. She agreed and said she missed her sty and her trough. A bucket would do, a bucket full of chestnuts with butter and salt. She shook more crumbs off her new coat. She felt good about the paper bags full of clothes they were carrying. She liked the clothes and the thought of wearing them, and she liked the crackling sound the bags made against her legs. Bags full of presents. Her own.

That night they had their first dinner party with his friends. He picked her up at eight o'clock, pleased with the gold-lined evening cape she wore; it left room for her eccentricity and fitted his dreams. A dining room had been reserved at the Ritz. All white flowers, all white porcelain, waiters dressed in white.

She was greeted with ceremonial warmth and air-kissed. They sat down to dinner. A series of plates arrived with meat or fish in the shape of flowers, or little towers of peeled and disembowelled potatos. It all looked good and left plenty of space for long intellectual discussion.

There was a lot of laughter behind napkins about the mistress of the President, a formidable lady in charge of one of the most important museums in Paris – all inside jokes, of course. She listened to their voices and pitched them in the middle of a scale. As long as they hovered around A they were pleasantly bearable, but if they were to reach B flat, boredom would strike. More wine, a toast to the mistress of the President, she ventured to say. A communal stare in her direction, a reluctant toast, a slight *refroidissement* and then the conversation bounced back into Parisian life.

There was some dancing going on in the next room. They all agreed with her that it was much better than dessert, that after such a sumptuous meal a bit of exercise could and should be *de rigueur*. She felt she had to dance, shake them off in a wild rhythm. The band was good enough, trendy enough for the American hotel guests to dance to, good enough to make a show of herself. He noticed her sweating, her hair swaying, sticking to her excited face.

In the cloakroom she found towels. She stayed long enough to cool down, to give her new friends some time to talk about her, and then reappeared, calm and perfectly made-up, to shake hands for goodbyes and to blow kisses. He took her arm, pinched her gently as if he wanted to get it out of her, her opinion of his friends. He was curious, he wanted to know her. Let's talk in the taxi, he said.

But she wanted to walk home, show her cape to the people of the night. So they walked through the clear darkness, admiring the architecture, doing a bit of dancing on the way until they reached the Place de la Concorde. She stopped and pointed out a huge oval window, fully lit, on the other side of the Seine. That used to be the writer de Montherlant's apartment, and that was where she wanted to live. Look, the books are already there. She climbed on to the edge of the big fountain in the centre of the Place to have a better look and then on to a statue, a satyr. She liked the satyr, she said that was her, that next time she got a new passport she would give that as her profession: satyr. And then she jumped. He hadn't noticed that they had been followed by merry wanderers who wanted to share in their fun. Soon the fountain was crowded with wet tuxedos and mermaids in evening gowns, all musicians returning from a gig.

She said he was not to be afraid, because he was the only dry one. She had discovered a mad violinist friend in the crowd and they were going to get dry in his hotel nearby. Hotel Crillon, was where he stayed now that he played with a pop band. They all went to his suite. There was a piano.

While the wet crowd stripped, he read through some scores. The violinist joined them, stark naked, his shrivelled prick hopping along to a Kreisler tune. She was dressed in a shawl, stretched out on the bed. When the music was over she clapped her hands and demanded champagne and a madrigal to be sung by the singers that were present. And she got what she wanted. Monteverdi singing in his ears while he watched the naked ones dress themselves in their full voices. While the nymph in the song was sad, his nymph splashed champagne over her feet and had her toes sucked by the violinist. He is allowed to do it, she said. He is a Levi, he is a king, the Levis were all kings.

That was it, the thing about the guy's prick, it wasn't shrivelled, it was circumcised. No wonder he was good at Kreisler. Jews were always into show-off tunes. He tapped the naked shoulder of the toe-sucker and suggested that it was his turn.

But she was done and announced it was time to go. They got a ride from a young man who introduced himself as the designer P. She yawned and told him she had just bought some of his stuff. Tonight at the party, had she been wearing his clothes, he wanted to know. Party? Yes, yes, she said, and then afterwards she had taken them off and had partied. And that had been real.

Loth wanted to know more about her family. But they were going to his parents; what about them? It was a long ride to his parents' country house, so he might as well tell.

Loth's grandfather had died when his father was five years old, and his father had been an only child, living in a huge empty house. His grandmother was always ailing and had withdrawn to her chambers. There was a library full of stiffly bound books where he read with his governess. There was tasteless food served by the butler in the empty dining room. His mother did not approve of spices; she thought they caused indigestion. The walls in the house were painted in washed-out yellow and hung with a number of awkward portraits. Art costs money and money was not to be wasted. He loved the tall windows and the view of the mountains and lake. When he was able to imagine that the view had taken over the stillness of the living room he felt happy. He grew up going from the house in the city to the country residence. Through his social contacts he developed a taste for the visual arts. When he was old enough to travel on his own he combined his visits to well-connected friends in foreign places, with visits to art galleries and museums. He started to collect paintings. He had never enjoyed sharing them with others. He was a loner who appreciated his background and had no problem in conforming to its ideas and standards. Then there was the young woman he wanted to share his art collection with. She was also an only child. And neither of her parents approved of spicy food. They had a lot in common. There was a wedding with guests, flowers, crystal and porcelain. The dress was Schiaparelli, the lace was hereditary. Of course. They were both short of words, avoided conversation. Even when their only child was born they kept it that way. On the long trips they took together to buy art, approval or disapproval was silent. A slight movement of the head or hand and the new artwork was acquired. Upstairs, the ailing grandmother kept talking to her only grandson. Why waste money on painting when you can listen to music for free? He sat with his grandmother for hours in the old house with the tall windows and the mesmerising view and listened to her radio or gramophone. She made him play the grand piano for her downstairs. She made him leave her bedroom door open so she could hear that he was alive. His parents quietly approved of the music. He could have it. He could have everything. The excellent school, later the Ecole Normale, and entertaining glamorous girls if he so wished. Just bring them home for a short visit. They had enough conversation for a short visit.

He yawned and demanded more details about her family.

Not her brother. Her brother was respectable and living a normal life with reasonable people. Only his cooking was worth mentioning. Her father had already been famous when he was young. A revolutionary who portrayed the suffering of his fellow countrymen on his large canvasses. She knew little about his childhood; he had never told her. From his postwar paintings she knew about the shadow of the lamp on the dining table and the absence of his parents and sister in the darkness behind the lamp.

He had always emphasized the fact that he was not a Jewish artist, just an artist who happened to use war and its consequences for material. Although he had been brought up with Hebrew and the traditional feasts, his was not a religious background. In fact it did not occur to him that being Jewish meant anything until, eight years old, he was walking the narrow streets of his city with his sister and was offered an apple by a woman who was hanging out of her window. He accepted, broke the apple in half and gave one half to his sister. The woman started shouting at him not to give that little

Jewess any of his apple. His sister had dark hair and dark eyes; he was blond and blue-eyed. The children had stared at each other in amazement and then ran away giggling.

The children had supported each other a lot in their artistic ambitions. Their mother, the daughter of a rich tailor, was a bitter woman. She was lazy and despised her husband for being a dreamer and not earning a living that could provide her with more then one servant. Her husband, the descendant of a long line of impoverished, red-haired Polish rabbis, liked to withdraw into his books after he had closed his little shop. Selling, whether shoes, soaps, typewriters, thermal underwear or ten other varieties of goods, was not his strong point. Eventually he settled for a deli where he liked chatting from behind the counter to the elegant clientele that came in late at night after a dance or concert. Fresh sandwiches with hot pastrami and chopped liver, pickles and a dash of hot sauerkraut and mustard were his speciality. While his customers ate he loved to show them a medal he had won as a boy. A medal from the state for being the best student of the year. He knew they laughed at him and he didn't care. He had learned, and still learned, things they knew nothing about, these empty headed partygoers. Blond gentiles, whose illiterate ancestors were crawling around in the mud when his were learning the Books and writing the Commentaries.

He couldn't pay for his son to go to school, so he got him a sweeping job in a diamond office. The boss of the diamond office gave the fourteen-year-old pen and paper and asked him to write a letter for him. The boy was ready to do this, but the black pen made him draw a diamond cutter at work surrounded by diamond dust. His boss did not get angry; he sent the boy to the atelier of a famous painter. That is how he learned his skills; in the morning he would sweep and in the afternoon he would paint. By the time he was nineteen his paintings made money and he had his own dealer. Together with his sister, who lived with a German actor, they were popular in bohemian circles. His sister played the piano and he seduced young blondes or redheads. His favourites.

He and his sister mixed with the German artists fleeing the Nazi regime, quoting poetry, broadening their skills, feeding on the knowledge of their erudite friends, and sometimes joining their father late at night in the shop to help him out with the sandwiches. They shaped themselves according to the wisdom and humour of a people they had never known, went on to move into bohemia and declared themselves assimilated. Nothing was left of their Judaism.

They were diamond dust.

Her father was sparkling at his peak, a famous twenty-five-year old, when he was told to sew a yellow star over his heart. He never did.

To protect himself from the racial laws, he married a Christian lesbian and lived with her and her girlfriend, who were both morphine addicts. Even when he had to go into hiding in the later war years, they expected him to get them their drugs from somewhere. He did. He went out into a world full of soldiers, a small blond man, to provide for their addiction.

Now, decades later, the sweat pours out of him sometimes, for no apparent reason. It is the fear he had suppressed back then, suddenly surfacing.

Postwar followed in one long period, a massive past that grew painfully into a future with a new family. His fame continued quietly in the shape of financial support from collectors. He picked up a few prizes; there were a few parties in his honour which he liked to endure in the company of attractive women. From the outside world artists would appear on his doorstep and share drinks or a meal with his family. His children got used to men dressed as tramps who enjoyed loud cursing and singing and who made drawings of them. Or portraits they would later discover, staring at their own childhood faces, hanging on the wall of some museum. There were exhibitions abroad and visits to the royal family of their country to admire a work created by their father on a regal wall. The children remembered the stale sandwiches provided at such visits. She still remembered having to play the violin for some princess or other, in shoes that hurt. And her father, his head slightly bent, talking and joking in the world that surrounded him, but that he never really seemed to perceive.

She never saw him cry. Until one afternoon somebody rang the front doorbell. An unusual sound, as people usually came to the back door of their house and knocked.

She was small, followed him to the door, hid behind his legs. When he opened the door the light that fell into the hall surprised her. Bright and beckoning her to go outside and play. Her father sent the man at the door away. He was holding a piece of paper in his hand, she could see names on it in handwriting. Capital punishment, her father said, he was against it, never take another man's life away, not even an evil life. There was an old Jewish tale he said, a myth it was called, that somewhere out there the souls of the world were being sent out and if you killed a man you took his soul and it might be an evil soul and it might be sent out again. He left the door open and stroked her head, and told her he could not sign to protest against this execution. They had asked him to help save a life, the life of an evil man, a man who had betrayed her father's sister. She experienced her own silence while listening to him, she heard herself taking in his tears. He stood facing the light and cried, and let go of her, his child, for she wanted to go out and play with the others.

She heard Loth's mother ask whether he had visited that old Jew, the artist, your girlfriend's papa? She heard his faint answer. He knew she was listening, although she pretended to stroll around the living room with his father who explained where and when he had acquired his Picasso, his Kandinsky, his Klees and his newest: a Kiefer. There was no small phalanx, no bond between her and her Loth, against these white capitalists that were his parents, these anxious well-dressed frames.

They had stopped for a picnic in the woods by some stream. Nobody around to spy on their lovemaking. She had stripped off her clothes and pulled at his pants, breathless for an honest erection. But he would not show his genitals to an oak or a birch. She went cold, limp and opaque, no shine to her skin next to him, her voice muted by disbelief. Watched him walk the path back to the car. His loose jacket on his back, shoulders drawn up in defence.

He kept his long fingers on the steering wheel. Nature did not have any sex appeal he said. She laughed and hoped that her body was not part of nature.

The paintings gave her the wrong impression: she thought his parents respected art. But it was the value of their canvasses that made them smile and speak with admiration of the artist. There was a smell of death in their very designer house. It floated over the dishes while they ate dinner. She politely tried to ignore it and kept her gaze fixed on the tall windows, trying to think of the pure smell of the mountain air beyond the glass. He watched her pour water out of a ceramic jug, another Picasso as his father had just modestly mentioned, pour and forget that she was pouring, so everything was soaked. She did not apologize, just quoted Rilke's poem about pouring liquids out over a dinner table. She laughed. Loth then noticed the smell of decay and felt free to mention it. Her faux pas was put aside. They all stood and searched the house for the smell that was growing stronger.

At night the duvet covers were smooth and cold, and her body was drifting. She had left him for her favourite dreams. He was awake in the dark trying to remember why he had brought her here, rather than his former Greek girlfriend, the daughter of a shipping tycoon. He had told his parents that he was going to get married to this strange woman. She was changing so quickly, growing accustomed to his habits. He deeply loved her edgy feelings and exaggerated tastes. She seemed to splash them around a little less these days. She had started taking cover. Seemed to have ideas about perfect Parisian behaviour. Too much, nearly. Cultivated her looks with extravagance. His mother wanted to know whether her curls could be combed properly and also if Jewish nails always grew in such a crooked manner. A comb had been presented to her when she was shown their quarters. She didn't notice it. He heard her play her violin late into the night. He loved Bach.

It turned out to be a rat that had died under the floorboards. They found a maggot-infested corpse with a solid tail. The stench was unbearable; they opened windows and doors to let the air circulate and threw the rat into a ditch outside. She went to look at it, and saw how it had defended itself against death by pulling up its hind paws. She could feel the strength of their rigid kick, the sharp nails sticking out into the air, the front paws falling softly, abandoned to the other life. The tail was as good as new. God might use it again she thought.

Hundreds of white maggots were in a great hurry to rid the earth of this carcass. Theirs was hard labour. She felt an urge to draw. Her fiancé called through the garden. He walked up to her and let the cherry tree rain its blossom on him. For that she thought he came close to hope, close to a future for them.

Black pearls were not for a young woman. They threw a dark shine on to the wrinkled skin of the salesman. His hands held the delicate beads up before taking them away. She had never seen them before; their darkness attracted her attention. So many full windows had been shrugged at before she made an abrupt halt. Stern, a name that could have come from the cold countries; it reminded her of familiar faces from her childhood.

His hesitation disappeared as soon as he saw her ignorance was genuine and her taste unborn. Stern opened its doors to them. She went for the old man, bent and bespectacled, polishing the display cases with a large cloth. Why him? How would she know that this man, who was modest enough to walk around with a polishing cloth, was actually the owner of this shop? Loth knew the man, his family were regulars here and often discussed him. How lucky he had been to be able to buy a Stern franchise. He was an Italian refugee, of course, but they liked his manners as a salesperson.

His smile was kind and wise when he showed her the necklace and told her not to buy such a thing. She nodded like an obedient child and followed meekly in the direction of the engagement rings. Rubies, warm stones, a flame on her hands. Red gold setting, again with a sunny glow to them. She listened big-eyed and big-eared to his lyrical comment on the jewellery.

With a circle of red stones around her finger she accompanied Loth to the antique bookshops. The old streets of Geneva were famous for their book dealers. Along the steep streets of shining cobbles, lined with young trees. There was music coming from the shops filled with heaps of books and piles of scores. She thought she could smell parchment. She struggled along the narrow path searching for violin music. Obscure names, composers who had never been performed, she read through the scores and listened to the music they produced in her head. The paper of the ancient operatic scores felt rough beneath her hands.

Her fiancé bought first editions. His voice was dry as he haggled with the bookseller. The bookseller stood rubbing his hands, bent over as if suffering from severe stomach cramps, muttering a price that was immediately rejected by her lover. Huge amounts passed over the counter for these precious old scores. She stood and listened, clinging to the one score she had found and wanted. It turned out to be expensive, so it was her turn to look the seller in the eye and offer him half the amount he wanted. He treated her differently, smiled and let her have her way. She thought she had a bargain but her lover assured her that the old man had earned it back on him. Clever, he said to the bookseller. The man smiled again, encircled in the afternoon sunlight, and said the young lady would be honest with the music and that the young man would probably never use the scores but let them increase in value his already well-filled bookcases.

They all laughed, each for very different reasons. As she put her hand out to shake the old man's hand her ring sparkled. He held her hand and admired the stones. Ah, rubies from Brazil, he said.

9

Everything seemed to belong to my husband. The inherited Limoges, the silver, paintings and furniture. He very much wanted to keep my childhood quilt and a first edition of an Oscar Wilde book. I agreed to my minimized possessions. Two suitcases were enough to take back home, back to my parents' home.

Dressed defiantly in a tiger print mini-dress and fuchsia high heels, we dined outside on the Place Beaubourg before he drove me to the train station.

A definitive kiss from his tight lips. He waited until the train started moving and waved as if he had been told to. I waved back at a man I had been married to.

My father never mentioned my husband. My decision was my own business. What mattered was that I was happy and productive in my line of work.

My mother sighed a little and let my father do the talking while she was driving us home.

Something seemed to be bothering her. Had something happened, I wanted to know, standing in the living room with one of the cats in my arms.

Just a phone call, she said, from that Irishman she had met in my flat in the South, the one with the tall stories and the torn jacket. A talented young man. He had called, wanted to know when I arrived. Could I call him? He was here.

Within three days he was sitting on my parents' sofa, discussing painting with my father over many glasses of wine.

'At least he's a man,' was my father's only comment late that night as I gave him a goodnight kiss. Had I been married to something else? I lay pondering in my old bedroom. I dreamt that a dog with one green eye and one brown came to me and complained about its loss of hair. I woke up and dug out a photograph of my ex-husband. His hair was thick and wavy, his teeth perfect, his cheeks smooth. He stood, tall and slim, and smiled at me.

I couldn't sleep anymore. The attic rooms where I had spent so many years making and learning to make music were filled with voices and moving shadows. I went to the front room and sat looking down at the canal, at the water that pushed me back gently into the folds of other periods in my life.

How I had sat with my friends in the window, smoking pot, aiming the smoke at nothing at all and laughing until my throat hurt. Boys had to be beautiful, and be quickly discarded afterwards.

Falling for an older man, a man who insisted he was weak, every time I had ridden his twenty-five-year older body. A flat boat drifted by with its motor turned down to a gentle purr. It was filled with mud. A man with a grey cap and a long coat steered it out of sight under the next bridge. Did he know that I was sitting there looking at him? Is that why he looked up at the window? Had he heard the voice of one of my memories? And where was he taking that mud anyway? Surely something had to be buried underneath that mud, maybe bodies. It only took one man in a boat in the middle of the night to create this tale. I was going to tell people about it tomorrow. But what if the mud turned out to be just mud? Then I would be an even greater fool then I already was. Was I? To have left my house and life in Paris and now to be standing here in front of a reproduction of a Memling painting that I had hung on my wall years ago. A yellow monkey on horseback beside another horse. The horses were drinking from a clear stream.

The monkey looked so confident. I had spent a lot of time thinking about that monkey and his absurd self-assurance about his position in life. To be riding the ultimate horse, to make it drink and lead it. Which animal had I led up till now?

A balding dog.

I had spent my youth working hard and earning enough to buy beautiful clothes, books and scores, but for a long time now I hadn't had to think about rent, mortgages or bills that had to be paid. My husband had provided. I stayed in my childhood rooms and took on orchestral jobs abroad to avoid my Irish lover. He had decided to stay and move into some place on a canal in another city. Living off an arts grant and painting the greys of the Nordic winter seemed to keep him busy. We met sporadically during a period of about four months. I thought of getting a place of my own and paid a visit to the bank.

The three-piece-besuited manager frowned at a well-dressed

divorcee with a freelance job who wanted a loan. I was so young, he smiled a fat smile, surely I would soon hook another wealthy fish? I stared at him in naive disbelief and began to realize that I had never thought of asking my ex-husband for money. Surely I could provide for myself?

My black orchestral outfits were all designer and expensive and irritated some of the female members of various orchestras. Better go for solo work. My clothes seemed to do half the work for me at auditions. A toss of my long hair and a solid technique did the rest.

I should have left it at that. That night my lover collected me after a performance and took me to a restaurant. He suggested I move in with him. I looked at him and remembered his island. I looked at my love and my life and came up with all sorts of hard, rational arguments not to live with him. He cried while I suggested, quite coldly, trips abroad, a widening of his education. He was young enough. But he wanted a woman like me. A woman who loved her music that deeply and his work just as much. I did not know that women 'like me' existed.

We sat in silence. The food dried out and changed colour. I heard the trams go by, the bells when they stopped or warned a cyclist not to get too close. A strangely old-fashioned sound for modern transport.

I meant to encourage his talent. I started talking again while I watched his tears. I somewhat enjoyed this emotional outburst, like something from a Russian novel. But I wasn't ready for it.

For some time he stayed out of sight and made me miss him. And when that missing became acute, I found him drifting around the stage door late one night. I took him home with me.

He started working in my father's studio and left his dirty clothes on my bedroom floor.

This quickly turned into an unwanted routine for me. To hear him sit down and joke with my father at breakfast while I sorted out his mess upstairs. A new and degrading experience. But not enough to destroy our nights together.

At breakfast we would all lose ourselves in conversation and I would forget about his dirty socks on my bedroom floor.

My parents and I went on a short trip. He was to stay on his own in their house to work in my father's studio. As long as he didn't touch some pigment colours that were rare and hard to find, my father was quite happy for him to be there.

My parents liked the dunes, the yellows and faded green of helm. They were at peace in the small house on the beach that belonged to my brother, who was painfully clean and organized. I was restless without my violin and told them so. Late at night I lay in my narrow bed and listened to the waves composing Mahlerian crescendos and wide Beethoven symphonies, and scoring the sand in narrow squared patterns like some *oeuvre* by Bach. I romantically endured the sea of symphonies during half sleep, but Bach kept me awake. I started reconstructing the Goldberg variations in sand shapes, lines and water maps, and eventually their strict variety made me sleep.

On our way home I told my parents about my experience. I never told my lover. Him being so careless made me think more. Left me on my own to move deeper into my music and what my love for it meant.

The pigment paints were all gone. My father asked my lover if he had used them. No, he said, he hadn't touched them. But nobody else had access to the studio. My father asked him again why he had taken them. And again my lover said they weren't gone. 'Well,' my father said, 'then I must be mad or a liar.'

When I discovered some of the colours in his new paintings, I brought the subject up again. He didn't want to talk about it. But I did. How could I be such a nuisance and interfere with his work? Such arguing was a revelation to me. Was this Jesuit justice? Within a few minutes I had become the burdensome, over-inquisitive female who seemed to have no other purpose in life then to annoy him with unimportant questions.

I kept my mouth shut in order to open it again in the presence of my parents. He had used the pigments. Why did he not tell us? He kept quiet and announced in an angry tone that he did not want to talk about it. But we do, my father said. He acted as if we were torturing him. After all, a bit of paint was not the end of the world. No, but the makings of a fascist were.

That's what my father called him, from then on until he died: 'your fascist'.

10

Tiles hit the streets the day I moved in with him. Loose pages from my scores flew around the street and floated on the water in the canal. A storm raged while we pushed our bits and pieces of furniture up the narrow stairs. We had a small house with three floors connected by winding stairs. There was enough room for us to work and live. My parents had given me a piano. I could start teaching the violin and even accompany my pupils on the piano. The idea of pupils frightened me. Would I be able to help them find music in their playing?

We put the piano downstairs in a medium-sized dark room right off the street. People would be able to hear music coming from the house, but not the neighbours, who didn't use their ground floors as living space. It had never occurred to me before that I could disturb people with my playing. Neighbours had been scarce in my former existence. As had lack of heat. There was only one gas stove in the house. We lit it and decided to go for a walk down to the river while the house was heating up.

We struggled along in a turmoil of multicoloured leaves, moist smells of autumn and gasoline and our confused feelings about starting a life together. I held my fashionable coat closed with both hands and kept my head down against the force of the wind. Gael struggled on beside me. He never looked at me; it was always me looking at him, admiring his profile, loving. He didn't hold my hand, and he kept the pace going until we reached the river. We stood looking at the well-preserved houses, lived-in museums they seemed, warm, well-lit and filled with an overflow of luxurious cosiness. Centuries of comfort shone through the big windows. Nobody had curtains so we could see the people living their lives. Gael had been very quiet. 'I want you to know one thing,' he said. 'I am never going to support you.'

I hadn't given the matter a thought so I shrugged off the cold sensation his words gave me. The memory of them was already branded in, though, with a red-hot iron, with a voice that shrieked in my head.

When we returned there were two kittens in the house waiting for us in boxes. They were our children, he said, could I think of a name for them? They were both black.

I fixed something to eat in the tiny kitchen and listened to him talking and joking, bringing the house to life with his mad stories.

When his grant was finished, my friends found him a job teaching drawing at the Royal Academy and my father organized an exhibition of Irish painters with him as the central showpiece. He hated having a job but loved spending. Antique jewels appeared in little velvet boxes beside my plate. He would go to Ireland regularly and bring back cakes and salmon for all the neighbours.

They thanked him but found his generosity strange.

They tolerated him because I was there to put things right when he put the bin bags out at the wrong time, or left the keys in the door so people could come and rob us.

The bell would ring and some self-righteous neighbour would stand there holding up the keys like a freshly caught fish. Did I realize how dangerous all this was?

He left the keys in the door once too often when I was away on a short concert trip. When I came back all my jewellery was gone. Ah sure, they're only stuff, things, he said. That's how I started distancing myself from material things. I sold most of my clothes; they were hardly going to be of any use in bohemian society. I needed pots and jars and pans and kitchen tools, for I had to learn to cook for my man. (I had skipped that bit of my education up till now.) There was no heating in the kitchen but I soon discovered that cooking kept me warm. Big steaming pots of food were comforting.

The only problem was it took time. My life in that small house shrank to a life divided.

The practising, the teaching, the performing were one thing. The secret drawing and painting, and the lovemaking, were outside time. And then there was a big, big bag, as I liked to see it, that had to be refilled daily with chores. Once they were done and the bag was filled, my real life could start.

The chores were shared once a week with a cleaner straight out of Proust who loved to explain life to me while polishing. My man did not participate in any housekeeping duties. The urge for hygiene and order was mine and he did not wish to share my concerns or be annoyed by me about them.

Soon the little hammers of duty tapped away from morning till night. They did not tap hard enough, though.

In between teaching painfully untalented people in the morning I would run to the toilet and check to make sure there was no shit-covered paper strewn about the place by my man. He rarely flushed. Then I would rush upstairs to check that no pillows had been left leaning against the stove (the fire brigade had already visited us once). On my way up and down I would collect glasses and tins before I made it back to my workroom and the next pupil.

At noon my lover would stroll in and I had the endless task of answering phone calls from his workplace wanting to know where the fuck he was. He did his work well and kept them all going with funny stories, so they forgave him a lot. I would be in the kitchen preparing a shopping list or searching for my mail, which he usually threw under our bed. Bills disappeared and the phone grew mute. I felt guilty because I was not familiar with this kind of life, while he seemed to take it all in his stride.

My chats with the grocer and the baker exhausted me, the carrying of heavy groceries even more. In the afternoons I tried to spell out difficult scores, only to interrupt myself to prepare a meal if I had a concert at night. My lover had to eat and so did I. I would clear out the kitchen and pick up a few books from the floor marked with banana skin or the entrails of an apple or pear. By this time the chore bag would be nearly full; all negative energy was stored in there, and once it was closed it could be ignored.

I had organized an immense storage room for those bags in my brain. They were full of prehistorically big maggots that began eating their way through the rubbish. The gnawing was bearable as long as my lover brought me warm toast and coffee in bed in the morning and late at night on our big bed again, and sometimes with colleagues after concerts there would be wine and fries, cheeses and patés on crunchy crackers. Fingers and feet touching, fragile sensualities building up to the every-day stormy sex, talking love back into me. Into my life.

A leak in one of those bags carefully stowed away in my brain occurred during the time I was preparing for my first big break: the Bruch violin concerto played in the main concert hall.

Nerves plagued me during the first full rehearsal with the orchestra in the concert hall. The conductor was good and I started to relax, until I heard the dry ticking of the conductor's baton on his music stand. The silence full of interrupted notes was audible. I was standing beside the conductor with my face to the orchestra. The conductor beckoned me to turn around and there he stood. It took me a minute to realize who he was, what was he doing here. How did he get into our rehearsal room? Why disturb me? Something dreadful must have happened.

I jumped off the stage and walked towards him. He just stayed put. Had I some money, he wanted to know? They, a few friends and 'himself', as he said, had broken the window of my workroom back home. I was not to worry, he had had it repaired, called a glass service and all that, couldn't leave my piano and stuff out in the open. Just ran out of cash to pay the repairmen. I stumbled in the direction of my purse. No cash. In the meantime about eighty people sat staring at us. The conductor was kind. Did he need cash, was that the problem? He sorted him out, we had work to do. I did not see him leave. He had stopped existing for me.

The music brought me back, back home. It always did.

We went to a shop where he had seen the perfect dress for me. Gael's taste was impeccable and also beyond my imagination. The dress was what I wanted. He sat down in the shop and told me to try it on. It was expensive and perfect. I wanted it more now that I was wearing it. Had he saved up to buy me this? I told him that I wanted to buy it, but did not have the means. Well then, he said calmly, if you can't pay for it you can't have it. Pity you're fiddle-playing doesn't pay, he added with a slight smile. I didn't understand why he had brought me to the shop. Surely he knew that he had no money and that neither did I? Trying it on and realizing it was ideal for me should have been enough of a pleasure for me. A new form of sadism had been born. Instead of wanting to kill him, I wanted to punish him sexually. And myself as well.

I decided not to pay the rent and buy the dress. And that was the beginning of an obsession well known in Italy as *fare bella figura*. I started avoiding bills in order to look the part of a successful artist. I started sacrificing what is called reality for real art.

My concert ended with a crowd of ecstatic friends in my dressing room. My dress was spread out on the floor beside a sofa so it wouldn't crease. He was holding court with a glass of champagne in his hand, not that he cared for champagne, telling everybody how good I was and how glamorous I looked. I heard his dark voice separate from the rest. It made me look at him, observe the way he looked, his body language. I stared at his solid boots that were trampling around merrily on the delicate material of my dress. I said nothing, feeling empty and unable to act, but a friend shrieked and pulled him off it. It wasn't that important, he said, laughing loudly, it was only a dress.

The next day, though, I was happy about the praise in the newspapers. I was tired from the enormous physical effort and felt empty. On the phone my violin teacher suggested a drastic reduction in pupils, but that just wasn't possible.

I stood looking out aimlessly over the canal when the doorbell rang. My cleaner. Once a month she was allowed to penetrate my lover's workroom. I was still standing in front of the window waiting for the light to fade, thinking of the taste in my mouth, being nothing, when I heard her shriek. Reluctantly I went downstairs.

The maggots were for real this time. There were enormous heaps of half-eaten food, leftovers wriggling with maggots. I proceeded to help, dressed in an apron and plastic yellow gloves. Thinking still, but differently now, thinking how bored I was, cultivating my disgust about all this. Something had to be there, some kind of feeling had to be expressed. I was still alive.

He was furious, of course, that his room had been touched, but his fury was short-lived because he was happy about the exhibition he was going to have in a month's time. Happy because his friends were coming over from Ireland. About five of them would be staying with us.

I caught myself thinking about the food that I was going to cook, looking forward to seeing their happy, satisfied faces.

He worked hard, I said to my mother on the phone. He made me look at his work at all hours and if I didn't say anything he got angry, and then he got angrier because I bothered him with my presence.

I started screaming. I did admire his work but now it suddenly made me scream. Every brush stroke. I would wade out of his room dressed in his shapes and colours, forgetting to remember what I thought of it, only feeling the threat that I must, must realize he was great. I had always realized it; it had inspired my own work. I had never screamed at anyone before.

It took energy to calm down and return to my own business. I slammed the door of his workroom and came back with the small drawing I had been working on. His attitude immediately changed into genuine interest. Image on surface was his game, after all. He liked my attempt and even thought I should bring it out into the open. Try a small gallery, maybe. Plenty of those around. As long as I didn't try to push myself into his exhibition space.

A blond young man rang the doorbell. He had a Dickensian-looking document in his hand. He introduced himself as the tax bailiff and asked for my lover. We were not registered as living together, so I could easily say that I had nothing to do with him and that I would inquire about the problem. I took him upstairs and made him drink coffee while I promised to pass on the papers. Tax papers, unpaid tax.

The bailiff left the house a warm and comforted man. I phoned a few friends to see if I could organize a loan to pay off the tax debts.

It took a lot of Bourgogne and a good meal before I mentioned the bailiff to my lover. The debt could be paid. Mrs O, a friend of my mother, was willing to loan it to us. We had to pay it back. He leaned back in his chair, satisfied with the meal and his work, his dark eyes shining with a flaming energy, and declared that he was tired and couldn't be bothered at the moment. Sure enough he would take care of it in time. Lots of people had tax debts. I wanted to agree. He was perfectly right, it was all so pleasantly easy, the borrowing from people who were so stinking rich they didn't need the money anyway, and then the huge group of people in the same boat as us, the people with debts.

So when the bailiff came to our door again, I greeted him warmly, complimented him on his new hairdo and set out with him to the post office to pay my lover's debt.

The bailiff appreciated my concern for a friend.

At night we slept holding hands, with the dark shadow of the cats on the white eiderdown. Our bed had been nursing sleep for centuries, it was hidden in an alcove in the wall which used to have doors. The doors were gone when we moved in. But it was still a deep, dark womb that took us in for the night. The same dreams floated around for nights, pleasant and miraculous, soft and velvety, to be recounted in the late winter mornings like fairytales. Dreams that turned into recognizable shapes, like books with the right stories and a painting of the sea on the inner wall, a present for me from a Dutch landscape painter.

People talked in the street below, boats moved the water in the canal and cars slowly drove their humming engines up the steep bridges. Only the sound of the engines brought us back to the twentieth century. Our thoughts drifted between a seventeenth-century sleep and a modern awakening. Who could prove that the talking outside, unseen, was not a dialogue between a woman in a long dress, bonnet and shawl and a Jewish salesman? Her soapy voice and singsong accent, his answers thickly spoken, were not clear enough to be understood. His warm body was still floating in sleep. This was the body of a friend, a painter, a thief. This was the body that radiated warmth because it knew the Irish tale of the salmon. The salmon of wisdom had been tasted by this body and had acquired enough wisdom to exude its heat. The body had a voice, a strength of its own when it read out poems late at night. Poems that were still present in the morning. Words to travel with through the day. Through the centuries. No space for doubts.

Their names sounded poetic: Sean and Fingal, Diarmuid, Dave and Dara. Their work had quality, or so the press and the buyers thought. They all had a lot of hair and one set of clean underwear each. Barefoot, they insisted on showing me real Irish dancing on the night of their arrival. They lined up their hairy toes on the wooden floor and moved them around to the sound of a loud, scratchy tune. They were happy with their beers and the meal I had served. They all grabbed at the potatoes at the same time. I stood behind them with a serving spoon, helpless. Their voices were loud as they quoted their favourite lines in books, or discussed fellow artists. I noticed they were very respectful about my lover's work although he was the youngest of them all. I listened quietly, taking in their stories and gossip about their inner circles. Irish art was their main concern. Continental art, as they called it, was more or less a blur. Not that they didn't admire it; it just didn't have much of a place in their world. They groaned their appreciation of my food, thanked me copiously, and left me with the dishes. It was time for them to visit the town. I didn't mind not joining them that night, although I enjoyed their company. I cleaned up and went to bed, only to be woken at two in the morning by my lover who breathed over me that he loved me so much. There was a knock on the bedroom door from one of his friends. They demanded a tune from me. I liked this absurd notion that I could go straight from sleeping to playing, so I put on my shortest silk slip and went downstairs.

They cheered at whatever I played and started singing. I put my fiddle away but they kept going until the cold light of day. They fell down on the floor among the beacons of beer bottles and ashtrays, and clung to their coats for heat.

I attended their alcohol-fuelled lectures about their work in the arts centre with my parents and my friends. I was so proud of my lover that everybody laughed at me. Yes, they agreed he was good, good enough to live with a talented person like me. Meanwhile the talented person that I was went around the city with the painters to buy porn magazines. Their favourite was farm animal porn. That should be the right present for their neighbours, real farmers. Lovely pink pigs in suspender belts running around in the rain, splashing up tons of mud in the act once their farmer had caught them.

The magazines were later confiscated by Customs at Dublin Airport.

A minister and my father opened the exhibition. The right people came to admire and buy the paintings, while the artists flirted with the slender Nordic girls that served champagne. People dressed in designer rags spoke without a smile to my lover. Even if he was the one, they were the ones with the money; they were there to buy him. I enjoyed him roughing himself up, his voice booming about the hall telling them lies, telling them what they wanted to hear about Ireland. I don't think they even understood his English or what he was talking about. There was this pale girl, all in black, wearing uncomfortable-looking shoes, pushing her thin hips forward while she stood talking to him and then she pointed in my direction. I could just about hear her saying how much she hated me and did he know me? He said no he'd never met me, but if he did he promised he would hate me too. I waved at him behind her back. Somebody tapped my shoulder. I turned around and looked at the face of a chubby man, his cheeks moving softly while he spoke. If I was the woman who had left some work at his gallery, he was willing to exhibit it together with another young painter.

There was blood on the wall beside the guest bed, long, bright streaks like the beginning of an abstract painting. We knew the one who had slept in it loved young boys, we knew he had disappeared into the night and hadn't appeared at the breakfast table. He had left a note, saying he'd spent the money from the exhibition on Oriental kids. Now he was off to the East for more, thanks for everything and fuck Ireland. If he had fucked Ireland the night before, it had certainly bled a lot.

11

Rubies from Brazil, Burma emeralds, diamonds, she took to them as if they were being handed back to her, as if they had always belonged to her. Even her mother nodded when she saw the rings on her daughter's hands; they were definitely in the right place. From Switzerland? She wanted to know if the Nazi vaults had been emptied and her family's belongings returned. Loth told her he had had to pay for them and that her daughter was now writing to the Stern firm; she wanted them to design her wedding jewels to go with her dress. Good, her mother nodded again with that vacant look in her eyes, never inquiring about the price of things.

Her father was suddenly a connoisseur of stones because he had manhandled a broom at the age of fourteen in a diamond-cutting workshop. He abruptly interrupted his boring monologue about the art of diamond cutting to rush off to his studio, muttering all the while that he should have thought of it before.

At dinner he told them he had ordered diamond dust with which to cover a new work. She wanted it as a wedding present. Of course the painting was hers if that was what she wanted. He looked at his future son-in-law as if he hardly remembered his name. Did he want the painting too? Loth's effort to make himself visible was painful.

Loth suddenly announced that she had made her first recording from the score they had bought in Geneva. He had stolen her news and now wallowed in her parent's pleasure and gratitude. She went upstairs and came back with one of her new concert posters showing her in her Stern jewels, airbrushed into unreal beauty, her violin a mere tool.

Her parents nearly cried when they saw it: what a terrible poster, so vulgar, what did all those jewels have to do with her music? Why had she not asked her father to design something? My god, my god, they sighed, and shook their silver heads, looking shrunken and shocked at such a lapse in taste. She just laughed and agreed, grabbed a bottle and suggested a toast to all things ugly and beautiful. Her father drank and muttered until he was drunk enough to think of himself as Marlene Dietrich and insist upon singing one of her songs for them. While he shook his imagined blond locks and hid his eyes under false lashes they watched through a haze of tears of laughter. Her mother sang later, raw folk tunes that brought their life back and took Loth's bride-to-be with them.

She tried to make wild love to him that night and again he had to point out his limitations to her. Not in his heart. Only in his body.

It had all been a summer joke: her foaming green dress and flashy green stones, impossible heels and her even greener smile. They had been married in the sour company of his parents and the lively presence of her friends. The food nearly killed his French friends and her parents had joined the party as if they were relatives going to some distant cousin's funeral. Her mother drove Loth's parents to their hotel late that night, driving a little faster than she usually would. So she told Loth with a smile the next day as she saw them off.

Primroses everywhere around his country home, plenty of wild strawberries on the kitchen table, gifts from the neighbours. When they arrived, a married couple now, they forgot about honey and wine. The hours were filled with music. He drove her hard, for he had plans for her. At the end of their summer she had to be ready for an international competition.

She won a prize in the chamber music section of the competition and received an offer to play in a southern city. She was a musician again, alone, with foreign streets to walk along and foreign lives to meet. She was going to come home to him every second week.

He kissed his wife goodbye. Somebody took a Polaroid. He was embarrassed by the tears in his eyes. When she looked at the picture in the train she noticed how long her hair was. It had grown.

Letters or phone calls were not his forte, but when she was at home she wore her stones and made careful love to him after a performance or a *grande visite*, as she used to call their social outings. There were enough elegant phrases and silences for them to continue their marriage as it was: lived from a safe distance. And when she came back she threw herself even more into the tastes of the town. She lost all superfluous weight, learning a most important lesson: if you can afford all the food in the world, you don't eat it. Her nose was slightly too big, but apart from that he found her quite flawless. She became more and more what she believed he wanted her to be.

She confined her dreams to her music. It was her poem, her passion that he respected, and as long as she followed his rules he would continue to respect her true love.

But she left him, with her cases and a few jewels, a wedding ring and all her scores. She gave him a drawing of a dead rat half-consumed by maggots.

He told her to keep away from the Irishman. He told her that in his circles divorce was not the done thing. There was enough room for this other man. Nothing had to change. She was going to take her music to a place where there were no melodies. He knew what her music needed. She listened to him creating her mythical life. She listened to his anger. She forgave him for saying it in the end, that his parents were right about her. He never suggested giving her money, neither did she ask for it. He told her he loved her.

12

It was a sad summer I had, the year of my thirtieth birthday. I loved getting presents and letters and celebrating my birthday deep into the night with my friends. Instead, I retreated to my parent's house for the summer. My lover had rented out our house and gone to work on his paintings in Ireland, taking the earnings of his exhibition and the rent with him. I got to mind the cats, and over the summer learned their language. I read his daily letters in smudgy handwriting. I looked at my face in the newspaper when my exhibition was announced and felt proud of myself. My father was ecstatic, and brutally dismissed my regrets that my 'fascist' wasn't there to celebrate with me. He would be back anyway for the opening.

What did I need him for? I had my music, my art, many admirers. I had my mother and father, who were all-understanding. And I was beginning to make enemies, which meant my name was beginning to be heard in the art world.

I was being a good sport. I started jogging in the early mornings, eyeing the flab on my legs, pounding out images over the asphalt, the grass, while hanging my own paintings, looking meagre, in the lush trees. I pounded my way through his absence. I had to understand the goodness of being me.

I took a bottle of vodka to bed with me. One glass had been the peak of my drinking, but it was my birthday and I was going to celebrate with alcohol.

Summer life was overrated.

Come cat, come back to me black cat. Have you seen him looking for me? My black cat comes, came back black. His tail round the street corner in the dark, his voice the only visible one. Lets himself be picked up and brought home. Together they came, my lover and cat, black hair and yellow eyes.

He was back, wrapped in splendid egotism. He had a red phase, he told me, and that was all. No need to disturb him. But I did.

The house needed some care after the summer so I went down on my hands and knees to work away with a brush in the hallway instead of going to a rehearsal as planned. I couldn't live with the caked-in footsteps and the smell of tomcats. He came out of his studio, screaming that I should be at a rehearsal, shouting that he could hear me using the brush and did I not realize that he was going to get rich with this series of red paintings he was working on? His voice echoed roughly against the clean tiles. Of course my lover was right; I should have gone out with my fiddle to make a bit of money while he was creating his fame and fortune. I felt guilty, splashing lots of water on the tiles. I did not love him enough, did not respect, admire enough, I kept thinking while I scrubbed the dirty steps one by one. I fixed him a great meal to make him forget. We threw the brush out of the window, had our meal and used the table for sex. It was the meal that got me pregnant.

Now let me play something for you, a lullaby maybe?

He took a studio outside the house and decided to give up his job for a more lucrative freelance existence. I would have to work harder now that I would have my child to support and a babysitter when I was away. Responsibilities rained on our disorganized lives. I found a new agent, the kind that rings at six in the morning for a replacement job and uses the same cold and formal tone to greet you, discuss your fees and provide you with details about the repertoire you're supposed to play. The money was good.

Gael helped me choose clothes that would hide my bump at the first night of my exhibition. And he spoke warmly of my work, although he talked more about his own. We smiled for a magazine photographer. I had the feeling I was looking through smoke-coloured glass and could see my breath on it but couldn't wipe it off. My paintings on the wall didn't matter anymore. There was only the silence between me and everyone else in the room.

13

His house is a temple and he has to provide for them, the ones sharing his faith in his temple. He has a wife called Laxmi. She is the wife of the Hindu Provider. And he is that now. He has seen her with the cats, sharing their paws, growing black arms, six of them already with sharp nails to get hold of him. More arms growing in her belly, arms that will grab him at birth and demand to be provided for. It is to the cold country that he brought her because she was going to provide for him there. Or so he thought. He did not know then that her name was Laxmi. She changed her name when she changed the beautiful coloured clothes she used to wear for the simple wrappings of the moderate. He had to leave his colours behind and cross every bridge in the new city to find it: the perfect grey. The transparent steel of the ice, the cracked ice like a non-colour, a diamond cut in the wrong place. The water covering his sleep, like a dark blanket covering his head so he could not get away. He had hoped she would serve him until he had painted the perfect grey in the painting that would bring in gold. She kept him fed and clean, but she stole some of the grey for herself and her own paintings, and she went around with her instrument to come back with coins instead of notes. He asked the cats to speak to him and teach him how to provide, but they just wanted to be stroked until their round heads were silk. Like her, Laxmi the goddess, who wanted to be stroked to grow more arms in her belly. He wandered away from her in the hours, but couldn't keep away for days. Silk brushes like the cat's fur, that's what he was looking for, to smooth out her portrait. Laxmi the cat mother, the independent wife dependent on the provider. He wanted to paint himself in his temple, but he did not know where he was or who she was. They were both asleep in this country. And so were the little big people he met who shook their clean fingers at him silently, voicelessly. To warn him against himself, not to try and reach the horizon, for even if he kept going, borrowing money for the road in Laxmi's name, he would never reach it here. It was flat and dissolved if you came too near. He was Hindu with her, living with the hope that she would provide the temple's candlelight, soft enough to make him see the warmth of grey.

Already he could not remember her as she should have been, a sensual symbol of his belief. A generous goddess of the rich earth. The grounds they walked together were frozen and she let him handle the biggest axe to open them and look for the riches she wanted, she needed. He had dreamt of her in the past as the woman who would fit inside all his paintings. And he had seen her in his life and felt her presence around him as a thick glove that would warm him and protect him from the others who wanted to be him and live his life. His hands had been free to paint in any religion; he did not mind turning them into Hindu hands as long as her name was not Laxmi. He promised he would paint whatever she wanted, even music, some bells, maybe, which would look so good that she could hear them. Most of all he wanted to paint the Provider for her to look at and take her gaze away from him. She said no to that painting; that was not to be. He could paint as much as he wanted but he could not paint himself away from her and the embrace of her arms. It was the only thing he recognized. The musk on her skin, the scent of a country he longed for.

When he first visited her temple she was surrounded by parents and he felt familiar with their images. She had asked him to look for her elsewhere. That was a time before her skin would lose its glow and her mouth would shrivel.

He stayed, and made her taste what would make her mouth at least contract if not shrivel: his idea of life. The days she began to suffer from being deprived of all her superfluous needs were good days for him. For he was teaching her, now entering her temple as a Hindu priest. Slowly he started to borrow her colours: blue came first. He took it from her, but she smiled and said she didn't mind because hers was a different blue. So he tried yellow and crimson and orange. All to the same effect, her smile and her belief. He said he was her husband. But he did not provide her with a new temple – theirs was a rented one. She didn't seem to mind that much. With the cats, her black allies, she sharpened her claws on whatever material was available. Sometimes she put her soft paw on another man's arm, and if he complained she would strike and cause him the pain of a deep cat's scratch.

They sold it in the shops: air and rags. She wasted money on them and came back to worship him, crippled with guilt and joy about her new possessions. Small things that she did not deserve. Because they do not deserve anything. And he was not the man to provide air and rags or even admiration for her. But she was right in one thing, to come and worship him.

14

Rembrandt was the name of the train that carried me through the Rhine valley, past the castles. Castles in France were alive in time, with a mixture of blood and wine flowing through the veins of their splendidly dressed inhabitants. Castles in Spain kept their walls rigid with religion. Castles in Ireland had the wind blowing fairytales through their ruined walls, but castles in Germany retained the threat of power and war.

I looked out of the window, my vision blurred with morning sickness, hoping to see the rock where the Lorelei had sat. 'I don't know why it is, *dass ich so traurig bin*,' I could hear my mother sing. The woman combing her golden hair to lure men to their death.

There was no money left in my purse when I arrived. I had been alone in the train. Because I was going to be paid in cash I hadn't brought any cards with me. I grabbed a taxi to the theatre, desperately hoping it would be paid for. Greetings and bowing, Very Respected Frau, the manager and conductor were waiting to escort me from the taxi and kindly paid the fare.

I made my way through the Bruch concerto and winked at the *kolnidrei*, the theme that evoked a synagogue lit by a thousand candles and the blowing of the horn to reunite all in friendship.

I took the night train back. Somebody with a sinister-sounding name paid me and accompanied me to the station. He threw a bodiless shadow over me and when the train left he still stood on the platform, and then he waved.

It happened too often. The carefully planned amount of money in my purse would be gone at the most painful of moments. I had to start improvising free trips on trains, hiding and sweating in toilets in case the conductor might find me, because I had to be in time for a concert or a recording and didn't have the cash to get there. Did he not understand that I couldn't work under those circumstances? But I could. I played better than before, and that fascinated me. Anxiety seemed to push me beyond my limits.

He admitted that he took the money from my purse. It was his as well. And it was not as if I was bringing in a lot. With all my teaching and trips he still earned more. Maybe I should take up translating, too; my French was good enough. I was pregnant so I needed to do something about it. He'd checked our bank account and saw that I spent too much on shoes. I protested that he bought them for me, but he got angry and told me not to annoy him. If I didn't want him to take money from my purse that was my problem. Not his.

I got heavier and nervous before leaving the house. There were the chores, there was the purse that had to be hidden and checked, there was the father-to-be of the baby who wanted a cheerful kiss before I took off on another miserably paid musical errand. And the child took off with me, listening all the time to the tunes I played for it.

There were my friends who shook their heads and said I shouldn't have a child. That was for different people who had their lives sorted out and deserved what I didn't.

He took to invisibility, my lover. Hours, days, he disappeared to roam the fields of his inspiration. He would come back with stories about his paintings and how they were going to improve our lives later on.

We got married when I had a belly to show to the world. Before the ceremony we took a short trip to Ireland to tell his parents. We had to stay in a hotel, for we were sinners and the neighbours did not approve of sins, especially not visible ones in the shape of a pregnant belly. Once more I sat for a couple of hours on the parental sofa and watched them pour lemonade into the cognac that I'd bought for them. The violation of the colour made me shiver. A deadly pink fluid seeped its way through the amber of the cognac and the drink disappeared loudly down their sinless throats. Meanwhile I was introduced to his twenty-year-old virginal sister who had a tan because she was just back from a Greek island where she'd probably screwed at least half of the young male population. But her hymen had grown back when she arrived home.

Mine was not blessed, which meant spending a tumultuous night above a disco sweating it out in polyester sheets and watching the various disco lights flash on the wall.

At eight-and-a-half months I sat down on stage and felt tired. A little extra pregnancy money from the State would be welcome, he said, now that I had a few free weeks I could stand in the queue and see to it. Being married meant being responsible for each other. In bed he recited the names of his favourite bailiffs to me and the baby that pushed its ass up my belly in his face.

Samuel was born to officially married taxpayers.

I had three weeks to spend full-time with him and the realization that I had given birth to death. Whenever the stupefying little bells of his bed toy played a simplified Schubert song, sadness would have all of me, a shapeless human being, a mother.

I would go to the window to count the seven bridges over the canal, seven rings that shaped a tunnelled view of light and water. Then I noticed the people on the bridges and they took me with them away from my life indoors.

My new husband was a possessive father and a baby-lover. He knew how to cuddle and cradle and shush an infant. His miraculous son was his gift for me, he said. I just laughed.

Again we slept long hours in the bed, which was now like an ark, with cats and baby coming along on the night trip. Friends brought flowers, presents and smiles. Mine were not the kind to give advice. His basket soon stood beside the cellist when I started rehearsing for a chamber music concert. We got a nanny from Ghana for Samuel. A singing Christian mother, she sang psalms all day long to my slumbering baby in a sling on her back. O Lord, O Lord. I could hear her from downstairs thundering God's praise into his baby ears.

The first six months of his daily life were hers. I was busy rushing my bow over my violin, enjoying Mozart and at times getting dizzy from playing too much lesser music. That first Christmas we took the train with baby Sam to France.

Friends were waiting for us at the station and drove us through the mountains to the forge they had converted into a house. We looked at the snow on the peaks and felt warm inside the car, warm with hope. There would be talking and music and lots of food, and all kinds of people to welcome us, including babies and greybeards, princes, or one prince at least, and bricklayers, though bricklayers who wrote novels on the side.

One whole wall of the house was occupied by the original blacksmith's fireplace. A red-haired man dressed in jodhpurs and riding boots leaned against the fireplace to warm his naked torso. He was discussing the merits of Napoleon Bonaparte's fighting skills with a pipe-smoking American seated at the long dining table. He was a Royalist, a King would have saved this country, it was good that the English had royalty and nobility they could send out to slay the French at Waterloo.

Samuel had been sleeping but now decided to scream for food. The two men noticed us in the corner of the huge kitchen and introduced themselves. A painter, huh, he said to my husband. The pipe-smoker's dark eyes were mad, he didn't like Picasso, the greatest flop of the twentieth century. My husband immediately agreed, just for the sake of the argument. I went up to the riding boots man who introduced himself as Napoleon. Still have some running to do, care to join me before it gets dark? I declined the offer and he was gone. We saw his very white skin on the mountain road under a freezing sun, running to his next battle. Our host arrived amidst a crowd of barking truffle dogs. He threw some bones on the floor and some truffles on the table for us. One of the dogs licked Samuel's hand. He howled with laughter. We had never heard him laugh like that before, a generous production of sound to express his delight.

While our host showed us our rooms we could hear Samuel giggling downstairs where he'd stayed with the pipe-smoking man. A happy baby, our host muttered while he poked the fire of our bedroom stove. It was a cold room filled with antique furniture, a huge bed covered with a great white feathered cloud of an eiderdown. I was shallow enough to be completely satisfied with it all. I was a merry young mother, ready for a meal with old and new friends, a hilarious baby and dogs that found us truffles for the *omelets truffee* we were about to consume. I was back, back again in a country that I loved. That I loved so much I had even married it for a while, mistaking the country for the man and the man for the country. We would be in the company of writers and painters, and the conversations would be colourful. Everybody would have forgotten the beginning and lost the end, but the words in between would sound good.

The days were filled with long walks and large meals, followed by mad dancing.

Our favoured pop and soul icons would scream their lungs out through the muffled speakers of a ghetto blaster that stood in the corner of the kitchen covered in dust. Samuel slept soundly most of the time, and when not sleeping he practised his laughter on a two-year-old girl. We were getting ready to shed the old year and welcome the new one with great elan.

Champagne bottles were cooling outside the sliding doors of the vaulted hall. It was a converted forge with long wooden tables, a piano and a harpsichord snug in a corner, and some large sofas and chairs that had obviously been ordered from a designer catalogue. They were like drifting islands under the ancient arches. We sprawled on them and proceeded to party. Whenever the sliding doors opened a new set of stars would arrive, bringing the cold night with them. People dressed in capes and hats or woollen bonnets, immediately confusing us with foreign languages after introducing themselves in hesitant French. I hopped from one group to the next, using my skill as an interpreter and generally displaying the thing my husband most abhorred: charm.

During the meal the courses were interrupted by poems, music and speeches. I played some tune accompanied by a friend on the harpsichord, and after the clapping sat down next to red-headed Napoleon. A particular dish attracted my attention, but he warned me off it. The salad might be good but I had to be aware of the fact that the bowl it was made in had been used for emergency peeing up in the cold bedrooms at night. Of course it had been thoroughly cleaned and if I were a true soldier I wouldn't mind. I had no talent for the army I assured him, and we drank to that.

The fireworks consisted of champagne corks sailing through the air at twelve o'clock. My husband, who had spent the evening twenty-five seats away from me in the company of some French mermaids, now needed saving. A Russian prince was on his knees in front of him and kept trying to kiss him passionately. He was crying drunken tears of gratitude, for my husband had just remembered, and had quoted, his favourite poem for him. Nothing missing, all sentences there, a saint, he is a saint, and I must kiss his lips. I dragged the prince over to the harpsichord and suggested he play. A storm of virtuoso notes blew over us. He bowed and again said he had played for my husband, for the poem. The object of his passion stood outside smoking a cigar. He couldn't stand the sound of the harpsichord.

I went upstairs to see if my baby was all right. He was fast asleep, oblivious to the party. I walked through the room next door to look out of the window. It was an empty room with just one big iron bed in it. I saw the modest sparks of the village's fireworks before I saw the snow-white cat. Napoleon was asleep on the bed, the cat asleep on his back. Of course his name wasn't Napoleon, that was the cat's name. He had come to claim it back for the new year. He opened his eyes and looked at me to make sure that I noticed that the name Napoleon had taken possession of its spotless fur body again.

On the first day of the new year we conquered a mountain with babies on our backs and watched the cities of the plain flooded by intense sunlight. Our breath was light in the winter air that smelled of wild herbs. I was happy.

On the third day of the new year we went back to our life in that Nordic city. My husband started working on a design job and I went to stay with my parents for a few days with baby Sam.

My father, sitting in his chair in the living room, started to sing when I came in. Did I know that song, he wanted to know? It was a song in Yiddish, a melancholy melody. It made him cry because it had been his sister's favourite, and now he would have to go to the ruins of the camp to sing it for her because it was her birthday. I was stupefied. I had never heard of the song or the birthday; I had never seen the tears of the past.

He got up and embraced me. Had I noticed all these people in his studio? They were waiting for him. He could not go in there any more, his Muse had left to join them. His work was done. I looked at him, aged in his transparent frame, his head with the heavy crown of hair. My father had started the journey back to his sister, back to their songs.

That night I heard the wind pulling at the windows. I got up and saw it, black, pressing against the cold glass, waiting to come in and spread itself. There was nobody in his studio, they were not sitting on the bed. Maybe they were busy building a boat for him, I suddenly thought. Then one night I smelled timber, and the second I heard a saw with a singing blade, the third night Samuel woke because of the loud hammering on the window, it sounded like a storm. My father died in the storm. But in the morning the sky was blue and still, so he could sail.

I never saw him dead because of the one Jewish law he agreed with: nobody was allowed to see the body once the soul had begun its journey.

His body was burned, and we said and heard a few things about his soul at the ceremony. My husband found the right words to say in public about my father's death. In private he was quiet and painted his painting for me, the painting of my father. It was good, in the end so good that he sold it for a lot of money.

I now want to play you this song, a Yiddish song. *Yisgaddal.* A prayer for the dead.

15

It was the portrait of my father that got him an invitation to come to New York, give a few talks about his work at Columbia University and live in an atelier cum apartment in the East Village for a month. He wanted me to come along and leave Samuel with my mother. She agreed and we brought our baby over to her house near the woods and the sea. My parents had moved there a few years before, back to the village where I was born. I liked the idea of Samuel and my mother making themselves popular with the locals. We left them with a lot of kisses and flew to the United States.

Without Samuel and the familiar walls of my own home, walking up and down the unknown, with the buildings leaning over me, I felt the death of my father far more acutely. While my husband was holding court with admirers and students I followed the streets of a city in turmoil, and kept hearing footsteps behind me. They were nearly inaudible, as if somebody was wearing socks over his shoes and stepping in exactly the same spot where I trod. All day long I hoped to hear breathing, a faint sign of life. There was nothing; all I knew was that my father was behind me. I was never the type to shed tears, but this feeling of his presence made me shaky. I trembled nervously under my skin. I made the tremble disappear in shops both big and small, where I enjoyed myself buying bags full of clothes for Sam. The poor child was going to have to change four times a day over the coming years. But then it came back: the tremble.

I sat down in Central Park and made drawings of the roller skaters. While I was drawing I started talking to my father who was sitting beside me. He seemed to like my work; his comments had always been dry and his compliments as scarce as snow in the desert. I wrote little stories beside my drawings for Samuel, for later. I was enjoying the wild gear the skaters were wearing and was irritated by my nervousness. I started speaking loudly.

I promise, I said, I promise I will look after mother. I know, I said, I know that you did not leave her anything. I will, I said, I will.

My mother had nothing but a meagre state pension. She could only continue to live in her house if her family paid for everything. I never gave it a second thought; she would stay in her own house until she died. My brother did not agree. A rational man, he explained to me in the patient tone doctors use for eccentrics, marginal types and the obstinate like me, that the state could provide my mother with a room or a small flat, and that she could survive. This was not about survival, but, then again, a doctor wants people to survive. Besides, my brother and his wife had just acquired a second home and his wife had given up her job as an accountant to be with the children, so he had no spare money. Before he had finished his reasonable argument I had fallen asleep with my head on his scrubbed pine table.

I woke up from that sleep in Central Park with an apple-green bird skating right in front of me. My father had gone and I sat looking at my shoes. They weren't sneakers, and without sneakers I was just a tourist, so I went in search of some. They were bright yellow and soft and I was able to make a bouncy entrance into the auditorium where my husband's lecture was taking place. It was full of students, pimply, surly-faced, greasy-haired, uniformly dressed, not daring to show a glimpse of eagerness to learn.

My husband's voice sounded lower than usual. I closed my eyes and listened with admiration. With love. Afterwards he had to be King and talk to the young people who had suddenly become animated. I sat in the back row and waited. A male student came up to me, excited about the fact that I was the painter's wife. He wanted to know if I was also Irish. When I said no he turned abruptly and walked away.

Being Irish in America was different from being a Jew in America. If you were Irish you had a chance of becoming President; if you were Jewish you still had a chance, a small one, of being refused entrance to a club or a building where you wanted to rent or buy an apartment. My husband often forgot to introduce me to the people around him at exhibitions and parties. When I mentioned something about a drawing technique I used to a famous painter we had just met, my husband took me aside and said I had to understand that everything was about him now. So no talking about my drawings or, indeed, my fiddle work. After a week of this regime I decided to go home. I had hoped he would help me mourn but when I mentioned my father's death he just said we all have to go some time or other. I talked to my mother on the phone and she persuaded me to stay and maybe do some auditions. I let my husband be and worked on some small paintings and a few violin concertos for auditions. An audition with The Great Conductor was arranged. But when the day came and I rang his doorbell, a dainty dandy opened the door and apologized for the Maestro: he was in bed with a terrible flu.

Play it for us then, the new painter friend of my husband said when I joined him for dinner at his house. So I played my life in New York and what was waiting for me at the other side of the ocean. If whales can hear each other from so far away, then my Samuel could hear me too.

The painter was silent afterwards. Then he told my husband how lucky he was, he said surely my husband asked me to play for him all the time, imagine such luxury, living with sublime music day and night.

Sam was beginning to talk. And I was hanging out in strangely similar hotel rooms all over Europe. I was still not making enough money. I had enough to put a down payment on our house, enough to pay the girls who were taking care of Sam, but not enough for the clothes I could not resist. We'd all like something, was my husband's comment every time I bought something that was not strictly necessary for survival. My husband did help to support my mother, but, of course, Sam spent a lot of time with her in the countryside, we had our bedroom in her house and we used her car whenever we needed it. There were advantages to helping my mother. She respected his work and liked their endless discussions about books and art. He sometimes bought her a book she really wanted, which she would gracefully thank him for. His hair turned grey and he let his tummy sag. But I liked a grey wolf with a full belly and a well-fed erection underneath. In between his exploratory walks through the city he would work at commercial design work but rarely at his own paintings. From the outside world there were messengers who came to him demanding paintings and public appearances, but he decided to ignore them. He had enough to furnish his cocoon: his son, his cats, his wife and his dreams of the future helped him exist through the icy winters.

I had another, small, exhibition of my New York drawings. The house, the chores, the students, the effort, the music, the growing fear and incertitude, the painting and the lack of means it brought, all hung in a bundle somewhere far away, on a giant crooked tree that grew out of our minds. We lived safely in its shadow and spoke about it in a warm and reasonable manner to lull it into a false feeling of security.

All that was real were the vineyards we saw from the windows of the old farmhouse we rented for a pittance from a Parisian fan of mine. A woman I had met in a swimming pool in Paris, her fat body spilling out of a minuscule bikini. From the edge of the pool she shrieked at me, saying how she admired my work, how she had been to my last concert. I stood dripping chlorine and water on her and asked her whether she knew about a house for rent in the South. She had several, she said. She said I could have the one that belonged to her uncle the Admiral who had died at Monte Cassino and had left her a big old farm. It lacked luxury, and in return the rent was negligible.

My husband had seen her and refused to meet her for cocktails. She was a dyed blonde, and therefore he would not go. I forced him to come and soon the martinis made him drool over the pictures of her uncle's house.

We made it our own, made the cats climb the olive trees and sleep outside in nests of dried herbs, made the pump work to bring us clear water, and built a dam on the river to make it deeper. We saw them coming from the tower built in the thirteenth century: foreign cars, gleaming in the hot sun like insects from outer space, crawling along the path that led to the house.

I fed them all, our friends, from morning till night, and played with them in the water and on the mountains. Sam developed a love for horses and rode them whenever he could. My mother would spend weeks with us, teaching Sam how to dive, dancing until dawn on her sun-dried legs. She had met some old friends whom she'd known some sixty years or so ago, English boys who had settled in France in a valley of their own. Once she had knocked their straw hats off; now they knocked their old bones about and sang songs from their youth.

Every year my birthday was celebrated at the top of the highest mountain at midnight, with songs and poems and wine, sleeping under the same blanket of hot air and waking up with a wild horse breathing down my neck and a honey-brown chamois nibbling at my hair. My mother and one of her British friends would come up the mountain path on a tractor laden with birthday presents. The table on the mountain grass would be set with a damask tablecloth, imperial silver, Greek water jugs and a variety of chipped Rosenthal and Wedgwood porcelain. Wild lavender would be growing at our feet and Sam would be running towards me through the long grass; he was my husband's finest gift to me.

We began to work through the year just so that we could return to this place. My painter husband lived and laughed and told his jokes. The money still went missing from my purse and my letters still got lost. As my concerts became more important he seemed less impressed.

There was a day in London when I had to perform at one of the top venues and I tried to use an ATM. It was the first day of a full week of rehearsals and there was not a penny coming out of the machine. We had a joint account, and when I rang he said he needed the cash, he had taken it, could I not eat in my hotel? Could I not walk to my rehearsal? Even if this gig was paying well, I did not have the goods yet, did I, so I had to try and survive. The hotel had no restaurant, so I munched sandwiches and spent every minute in between rehearsals in my room sorting out what I was doing wrong. Another great empty question was my answer. At night it materialised and threatened me.

At home again, with a good review in my pocket, I handed over the presents and we acted as if I had done well.

I painted my anger on my first big canvas and sold it to a museum, earning more than before. But never more than him. And the rules remained: the person who brought in less money had to do more of the other, practical work: the chores. Even so, there was my very good madwoman, the cleaner.

There were still the summers with the siestas, when the three of us slept under the mulberry tree and nobody could touch us. Three bodies of love. Still the horses taking Sam for a ride and the rat in the well and the snake on the stairs and a loud song to scare it off, with the thunderstorms that flooded the kitchen and made us sing, and all our friends in the dark lit by candles.

While the fox played with the donkey, he said it to me. We sat on the terrace looking out over the valley in a glowing twilight and watched my mother and Sam race with the donkeys. Two friends of ours were in the kitchen cooking up some mysterious mushrooms and I was drinking Kir and eating pretzels. And when we saw the young fox play with the donkey, the scene turned Biblical. But then he said it: he wanted to move back to Ireland. He missed the strain of life, the rain, the deprivation.

Somehow I ate the mushrooms that tasted poisonous, Sam fell asleep on a couch with the dogs, my man got drunk, my mother was tired and I had to drive them home along narrow roads, the mountains standing in the pitch-dark like prehistoric shapes.

When we arrived I managed to open my car door and fall out in order to let the vomit flow.

16

He made them smile, the people in the offices, those that rang his doorbell and brought him papers. He told them about the fishing and they went along with his story, went with him to the green shores and the rocks in the dubious sunlight until they saw the silver streaks in the white water and forgot all about the papers because they wanted to catch these bold and free animals. He made them laugh, the people who had warned him on the phone that life needed to be lived in the way they had organized it. If not they would nail him. He invited them to his studio and told them about Maria in his paintings, about Laxmi, how he had invested in her music, supported her, how they should turn to her, she knew how to handle papers and questions about a practical life. He showed them the riders and the heroes in his drawings and brought colour to their pale faces. He brought them excitement, telling them about the people that lived underground and made them think that nothing mattered, centuries, countries, wars, the myth was carried on, that these stories were true, were poetry. They laughed and liked him until he closed the door on them. Then they would rush to spread more bad news about him. His lies were good, just as good as his stories, as the great poetry in his paintings.

At night he dreamt about the Great Fish, the one he caught although the Old Druid Fergus had forbidden it, and he grilled it and ate from the pink tinted meat and felt the glow. More wisdom came to him. He now knew. It was the way in which she had said it: come to me. She was the Banshee. She had cursed him to live his life in this country that was populated by people carrying wide wallets full of cards and money. Cowards that left half the whiskey in the bottle on a night out. Couples that sat in big rooms on designer furniture and talked about insurance and the price of houses to keep themselves and their friends entertained. People who got up early on the first summer morning to drive to their second home in a hot country, pretending to be modest in a second-hand car, off they went with a stash of extra insurance papers in the glove compartment.

He wanted to paint and to get the paint on the canvas he had to protect himself and to protect himself he had to tell the whole world lies, beautiful lies that sounded so much like the truth that the people from planet earth believed him. At least for a good while. Enough to be left alone with his painting. She took them from him. She held a mean mirror in front of him and stood in the silent hall where he had to share his life with her and her offspring. The boy he would feed with some Fish and make him see. She was the one that turned his gaze from his painting to the mirror. He heard her howling outside, panting in his ear when he lay awake in his bed and her beside him, warm and asleep. The whole alphabet of truth she possessed. But he had the Fish and the wisdom, and he could be the priest of evil gods if he wanted.

Yes, he could celebrate her the Banshee and give her a name even. Moira had his child raised by her mother. But her mother was weak now and losing her bewitching power. Soon he would sacrifice Moira to a greater being and offer him her stones. She would have to go naked and freeze her limbs. Still she carried that blinding light with her, it was so clear that even she could not see. Ban Shee, Ban Shee needed the darkness of death to discover his pain in his paintings. She held the lime-green snake that fled under her feet, she held the rat that could not bite and died. She wheeled him around on a fast lane from cold to hot and back, the landscape shook behind the windows of her foreign house. She made him talk to other painters and wear a worn straw hat and hide from the sun, walking with a bottle under his arm filled with the spirit. Among the gods they discussed he told the story of Moira the evil who wanted more of his seed to turn into her look-alike. She now had her demons to serve him, bang at his door for more, more, more.

She stood alone now, carrying death as a giant cape, taking it with her when she abandoned them to mourn on a foreign shore. He could make her hide in it, now the theme of her beloved song could be lived on his foreign shore. And nobody would listen. Let her sing and play over there. In darkness let me dwell...

17

A number of bailiffs called on me, all in search of the same thing. Again, I had no idea what they wanted from my husband. But I had no time to deal with them. My mother was dying.

Again I asked my brother to help financially – with the nursing, so she could die in her own home. But he said hospitals take good care of dying people, she had only a few months to go and besides he desperately needed a new Italian kitchen and had no means to waste on a private nurse. I cancelled my life for the last six weeks of hers. Sam was with his adoring father and his adoring nanny, living city and primary school life to the full. I could be missed at home, and in concert, for a while.

I drove her to the sea along the road in the dunes and she mentioned the sea light. I drove past the house where she had given birth to me and once again she told me the story. How warm it was and how my father and the doctor were celebrating with a glass of brandy at midnight, how she saw them standing outside, two triumphant small Jews lifting their glasses to life, laughing. The house we lived in was a present from one of my father's admirers. She talked and talked and filled the whole book of time again with stories and people I knew so well. At the beach we struggled down to a beach café where I left her sitting behind a glass windbreak. I waded through the sand to the sea and dipped my toes in the waves, afraid to turn around and look at her. I just stood and noted everything, the colour of the sky, the gulls with their broken song, the kisses of the light foam on my feet, endless, endlessly repeated, the stretch of white sand reflecting my blankness, because all my thoughts were leading up to the moment when I would turn to see my mother sitting there alone on the terrace.

She wore sunglasses and a straw hat, she was reading a book. I stared until she felt it, and waved at me as if I was a child.

Then she became my child. I washed her and read her favourite authors.

She had moved into my father's studio and had installed a hospital bed amongst his paintings and books. On the floor stood vases full of flowers that her friends brought in every day. I also brought her flowers and a new recording I had just finished. She kept her eyes closed, listened, and declared herself intensely satisfied. She had always been a stern critic and the approach of death had not tempered her judgement. She even refused to see some people she had mildly disliked in the past. Her body consumed itself, she could not eat and the day came when I was able to lift her up and carry her to her chair. She liked it and said I was strong. And I felt stupid and proud to be strong.

When my brother or a friend stayed for the day, I would drive home and collect clean clothes. I changed my rings and noticed a few had gone missing from my box.

Had I left them at my mother's? I forgot about this on my way back to her house.

She was still there laughing and joking with her old bohemian friends. They were my friends, too. We sat around her bed and talked about the good and the bad that had occurred in art and politics. My husband came to visit and loudly joined in any discussion. They liked him and admired his work; he fitted into their circle.

A few weeks before her death she said I should go to a concert or a play. So I went home and got dressed and looked for my rubies, earrings and necklace, which were gone. Had Sam and his friend been dressing up in them? He had never done such a thing. I asked him and made him nervous; he did not like things that went missing. My husband had no idea either and looked worried. Was there a thief among our visitors?

Again I let it be and hurried back to my mother the next morning. I had to tell her about Sam in detail. We looked at my father's drawings and went through the war years when she had been alone, hiding and starving. She waved it all away with her thin hand and sank into a morphine slumber. When she slept I practised in another room until she called me in for her daily concert. Music of her choice.

It happened that she asked for a piece to be played at her funeral. She was sorry to die so close to Christmas. With all the holiday dates coming up, it would be complicated to cremate her. She did not know that we had to pay for her funeral because nothing had been arranged by my father. The word 'money' rarely entered her vocabulary, she knew nothing about it and had dealt with her losses by cultivating a bitterness tinged with humour.

Sam came and held her hand, counting the brown spots on it. He was shy with her because she had shrunk so much. But her voice was the same and soon she made him laugh and got him to tell her a thing or two. He kissed her hand and said goodbye. His father took him home. I spoke to Sam on the phone the last week before her death and he asked me if I had found my rings and pretty things. Daddy, he said, Daddy thinks that it might be a ghost that took them and now I am frightened and sleep with him. I teased him and hung up. I sat beside the telephone for a long time. I wanted to talk to that ghost, to show it my fury.

We talked on the phone every day, my painter husband and I. He casually mentioned that he had found a few rings in the pocket of his jacket, a queer business he added, and then proceeded to ask about my mother's health. I announced that he'd better come over because she was not going to live another full day.

The wind hammered on the cold windows again, but the next morning the garden was white and my mother greeted me with a faint smile. The house was warm and I spent the afternoon reading and chatting with friends while she faded into her last sleep. A painter came to the door and asked if he was allowed to make a drawing of her.

He was an old friend so I let him in and gave him a glass of gin. He went into the studio and started drawing my mother's face. Again the doorbell rang and my husband came in, bringing snow on his coat into the house. He was hungry and wanted to eat. How was my mother, he asked, and blew a butterfly kiss on my cheek. My answer was dry and clear: she was going to be dead within the hour. Jaysus, he sipped from his wine, I didn't realize it was that bad. I heard him from the kitchen, yes, I muttered over the frying pan, it was that bad. I sat down and watched him eat his fries, and went to the studio to feel her hands and face turning cold. I came back, and before my husband had finished his food the painter called me. He was crying. I held a small mirror in front of her mouth and saw no reflection of life on it. She was dead.

I rang my brother and some friends who immediately came over to have a drink with us. My husband rang the funeral home and had a bizarrely jolly talk with the undertaker. There was no room for my mother over there, the fridge was full because of the holidays. Better leave her at home and open all the windows, as it was freezing out. We laughed and I hoped to hear her laugh. But she didn't, and when I went to turn off the lights and open the windows in the studio I felt the ghost's cold claws grabbing at me, coming in so quickly from outside. How could she have defended herself against this? It rushed out again and took my home along into the winter's night.

Where is Grandmama going? Samuel wanted to know when the coffin went down to be burned. Our whole world was silenced under the white shield of snow, frozen snow with stars that winked at the sun.

More went missing in the house. Sam saw his granny's ghost and couldn't sleep. The ghosts had taken over, we had to give them what they wanted: a party. Everybody came and made a drawing of his favourite ghost to be hung on the party wall. There were ghost cakes and ghost clothes and a choir to ban the ghosts. It worked and Sam was again able to sleep. I was lost in work and papers that needed to be ordered, and her absence whenever I tried to phone her. Her silence was slowly choking me.

I took a train through the country to see spiritualists in three ugly cities. The first came from Africa, banged the drums, lit incense sticks, and chanted and waved his large sleeves while freeing his armpits of their fantastic odour. Orbu, his private god, said all was well. I left with an empty purse. The second was a woman who rode her bicycle around the room and knocked over the family photographs, the one that fell nearest to me told her what she needed to know. I had to cross the water, she said. I went downstairs, unlocked my bike and crossed the first bridge over a canal, feeling none the wiser. The third, another man, asked me one question and stared at me for half an hour without speaking. It was in the house, he said, somebody in the house took my jewellery.

I asked my devoted cleaner and she started to cry. Then I asked the wall. It did not answer. Not his hands, my husband's, not even Sam's little hands could distract me from the loss of her. My mother. I flew to a remote coast where I sat on the rocks and spent my days in the company of pelicans that offered me fish once they got to know me. Their compassion made me cry for the first time. Tears of salt added to the salt of that Pacific ocean, as indifferent to any of this as my sea at home.

No reason for you to stay here any more, he said, when I came home with a bandaged leg. Let's move to Ireland my country, but you will have to take second place.

He had had a great offer from an art dealer called Antonio and was all excited about it.

My reviews in European and international newspapers and television appearances were all very well, but my work didn't really bring in the big money, did it? We had to move and he had to start his series of paintings that were going to make us rich.

Before taking second place I had to appear in a summer festival, and my leg was bothering me.

When I went to see the doctor he complained that he hadn't been paid and wouldn't treat me. During the last months I had neglected the insurance papers and hoped that my painter husband would take care of the administration while I took care of my mother. But he hadn't. There were the phone calls, there were the threats, the phone was cut off. There was the crowd of bailiffs again. So when I came home from the doctor he told me he had sold our house. All I needed to do was to sign the contract. Great, gone in one day and so were his debts. *Our* debts, he stressed, *our* debts. My leg got worse as the concert drew nearer. My husband laughed at the idea of a one-legged pretty violinist on stage. An excellent publicity stunt, he said.

I had developed gangrene. Friends and colleagues helped my slow recovery. All those I was going to leave behind. Why was I going with him? To follow my angst and learn to ignore it. Because once a teacher had told me to seek impossible boundaries and find a greater depth behind them or a more beautiful life. And because he still held me ensnared in his web of love and lies and mysterious imagery. His hands, with his brush on a canvas, or on my body, could still banish the dullness, the greyness, with one touch, one dab of passion.

Listen to this ancient tune; in darkness let me dwell.

18

We discovered the path to the moon from the windows of our new home. It was a very empty home for the first months because none of our belongings had arrived. But there were windows everywhere filled with the views of the sea and a rocky island with the ruin of a castle on it. I told Sam that Isolde had lived there before she travelled to Brittany to find her great love. He had just read a version of the story in a children's book and stood on the deck in front of the house for hours looking out for her.

After our move my husband had gone back to the Nordic country to finish some work.

Sam and I were alone. I had no car so we investigated our new surroundings on foot. Sam had to explore a new language and the small school he went to.

We set out for the city centre to buy him a uniform, something that nobody had ever seen in Sam's country of birth. Uniform means the same, I explained to him on the train that moved like an ancient slug. People stared at us with our foreign brogue and funny clothes. We looked back at them, with their woollen hats and anoraks and shapeless shoes. They smiled at us and we smiled back to mirror their warmth.

Sam couldn't stop giggling in the big old-fashioned shop where a nun-like creature tried to sell us the leftover sizes of the uniforms, as we were late in the year. Trousers that hung around him in grey misery and a cardboard jumper with a V-neck, showing the collar of his equally deplorable shirt. I could not restrain the tears of laughter when I saw him dressed like that. Already I missed his bright T-shirts and jeans. It seemed as though he had to peel off the first layer of his pleasant freedom to be able to fit into the new system. At least his school had no religious hang-up as all the State schools seemed to have. Schools that pretended to be non-religious yet had nuns presiding over the grim buildings. They all said it meant nothing anymore. Nothing, mere habit. Like those non-believing friends of my husband, who got married in Church to please their parents and baptized their babies to please their family and the neighbours. Ach well. I liked to listen to the horn-blowing of the Kol Nidrei at Yom Kippur in the splendid Sephardic synagogue. And meet those lost souls afterwards in the semi-darkness to listen to them commemorate my parents.

In the evening we stood, the two of us, in front of the kitchen window to see if the moon had already rolled out its silver carpet. He wanted to know what 'Catholic' meant. He said it with his back turned to me, keeping the moonlit sea path for himself. The place where his granny went every morning was a church for Catholics, I began my lame explanation. Granny was not Sam's favourite person, neither was his Da as he called the man who never spoke a word to him. He seemed to breathe cigarette smoke and kept a whole lot of televisions and a radio on full blast in his cramped house. The rare times he had been to visit, there were never any toys for him and granny insisted that apples were sour and bad for your digestion and that Sam should drink a drop of liquor when he had a bad cough. There were bags and bags of sweets and biscuits, and granny would talk for a long time without waiting for an answer, so he could eat the stuff till his belly burst. Even so, Catholic meant that you had no fun, watched TV and drank big glasses of burning water they called brandy or whiskey. It meant you went out in the rain in the morning and washed your face at the entrance of the Church and muttered some inaudible words while you kept your hands folded. I held him and whispered that the good thing was that if you were naughty you went to see a man in a dress and he would ask you to mutter some words called prayers and that was it; you were not a naughty boy any more. Punishment was only for those who did not know the words.

He stood thinking about the concept of religion while I built a fire in the living room.

The flames were good. I sat him down to tell him more. The flames were bad long ago, when the Catholic brothers wanted to burn your ancestors. We sat on the wooden floor and I drew a map of Europe for him and made a cross on Spain. There, it is still hot in that country where your grandfather's people came from. There are strong-smelling flowers and proud horses in the mountains. People like Muslims, you know, like our neighbours back home, and pious Jews, lived together in peace. They read each other's books and listened to each other's stories and they rode each other's horses and shared the wonderful sweet grapes that grew on their terraces.

One evening, maybe as moonlit and as sober as this one, you could only hear the turning of pages of the holy books like an insect beating its crackling wings in the dark.

Jews and Muslims alike were reading when the Christian brothers on their barb horses came and took the Muslims, to throw them in the sea. The king chose a queen. As a wedding gift their new queen wanted all the Jews out of their country. So they fled on their elegant Andalusian horses, you know, the ones that do the Spanish walk, and some stayed and were burned in the flames. Since then the Roman Catholic Church has ruled the country with the kings and queens. Your forefathers went north and continued to read their books. But we don't read those any more and that's a tale for later, my little pelican.

I felt I was alone, there was nobody any more who could so much as nod in approval or swear that I told the truth. Now this was my family.

He came with boxes and some of the furniture; it had been too expensive to bring everything. He came with a young woman who had to assist him with a huge canvas he was about to start working on. Now that he was home his mother rang and wanted to know if we were settled. Apart from the unpacking, we were. Help was not what family was for, I understood very quickly. I rediscovered it all while I unpacked, my own things and the few objects that my mother had left me. My painter husband and his assistant were working upstairs when I discovered the ghosts. They had shrunk to the size of little pieces of paper with numbers on them. All my lost jewels had been taken to the pawnbrokers by my husband. I started to scream and he stamped down the stairs to complain about the noise, to say that I was an embarrassment.

I held up the pieces of paper. How dare I touch his papers again. He had not asked me if he could take my jewels or told me after he had done the deed in order to protect me. And that was the end of it.

Could I now continue unpacking the books? And by the way, 'What's for dinner?'

My suitcase was waiting for me. My child watched me pack with anxious eyes.

But I couldn't leave. My life was here, now. I had to deal with it somehow.

The phone had been ringing for me, here on the island, to offer me some concerts. I had gladly accepted. The bush telegraph had warned the islanders that I was here. My husband was pleased. Pity the performing fees were so low, but I wasn't going to have much of a musical life here anyway. There was no tradition for such elitist business. Too expensive. The knot was tightening. I had spent so much time travelling that I'd hoped to spend more time with Sam and with my paintings. After my mother's death I wanted to fill the void with a new home life. But, of course, I had no students here and for the first time in my life found myself dependent on him.

I wasted time on the telephone looking for students and contacted a couple of violin teachers that I had heard about back home.

They came with a box of chocolates and sat at the edge of the decrepit sofa telling me nervously (they both burnt their lips with hot tea) that it was going to be very difficult for me, me being a stranger over here and all. And look at me with the house and the view and the nice husband. Why didn't I take it easy?

Taking it easy was definitely not what I wanted to do. The phone rang in the empty hall, a man's voice boomed down the line, as if he were standing in a field and had to master the elements in order to reach me. He invited me to his festival. It sounded good. Poetry, music, an exhibition by a fine painter, and, yes, he knew my husband, very impressed by his work, yes indeed, did I use his name then? No, I replied abruptly.

This was to be my first Irish gig. I travelled early in the morning and nearly forgot where I was going when the landscape took hold of me. It had wildness and mystery, and told a hard and cold tale that left me unsure of its beauty.

The organizer of the festival showed me the premises: I was to perform in a big pub together with a poet. I hadn't done that before. I wanted to make them forget their Guinness for a while. I rehearsed, went to my hotel to get rid of my stuff and walked the coastline for the rest of the afternoon. The sun made it look as if a lid had been lifted off it for a few hours and soon the lid would come down again to lock it up into a dark space.

Sam and his father were to come with the poet in his car. As I walked back to the hotel I could spot Sam jumping up and down in his red jacket.

I took my child to the hotel room and arranged for a babysitter. Nightlife was about to start, what with these writers and painters all around. They never stopped smoking or drinking during the reading or the music. Afterwards I went to pick up my fee from the organizer. The man smiled broadly, his face flushed from alcohol. Ah no, he had paid my husband, well you know, I sort of knew him from before, so I thought with him being your husband and all, I could give him your cheque, like, in his name.

There was only one street to stride along in fury, but a lot of pub doors to be opened and slammed shut again before I found him with his mates, drinking their pints.

Surely I should be at the hotel minding Sam instead of roaming the streets at night? They all grinned and showed their ugly teeth. My cheque, yes, he'd cashed it at the hotel desk, but he was more concerned about the child. How could I leave him alone?

I tried to explain that he should have arranged for the sitter to stay longer, and that I had been giving the concert and wanted my due, and a bit of fun afterwards. They all stared at me and patted him on the back, ah sure I was a hard woman.

The next day a white beach and burning blue sea cleansed us all to the bone. Sam, his father and the poet chased the wild horses while I was left with the soft wind sweeping patterns in the sand. There was nobody around; it was so empty that for a split second I imagined nothing had been written.

My pockets were empty when I stood on the ground of my homeland again. One small banknote was not going to get me through the week, and I'd left my bank card on the dining table back in Ireland. Not to worry, his assistant was arriving tomorrow and would bring me my card. He sounded like he was in a good mood on the phone, things were going well with Antonio his new art dealer. Pity he couldn't be with me for the opening of my exhibition but he was convinced I would have a good time on my own, with my friends and so on.

His assistant didn't bring my card. My husband hadn't mentioned it to her.

So I had my shared exhibition but couldn't have a good time with my friends. I did my publicity stints, being filmed with my violin in front of one of my paintings, wondering all the time how I was going to pay the fare back.

A sea canvas sold and the gallery gave me a generous advance. Enough to go home with.

Ireland, where my son was turning the weather and the language into a place to live. His teacher in school had red hair and looked like an Irish Setter when she walked with her long mane, holding hands with him on their way back from the playground. He came running to me when I collected him from school. The other parents all looked away, didn't seem interested in getting to know me. It was very cold in the house when we arrived. But my husband had a lot of warm kisses for me and good news. First we needed to clean up and then we would talk. No cleaner here; the raw chores were for me. I had been absent and the house had filled itself with dirty washing and piles of pots and plates. Tears splashed on the used burgundy of the carpet and my favourite shoes. How was my show? Did I have a good time despite the lack of wherewithal? I stood in the bedroom asking myself these questions. A few days of hard labour kept me warm, so it took time for me to realize that we had no longer had any heating. The gas had been turned off. It was freezing in the house.

I went about with a scarf over my head and wrapped Sam in layers of clothes.

Once the heating was back on I was in bed with pneumonia. A doctor came and had to be paid an exorbitant amount, nearly three times as much as at home. Gael was standing at the end of the bed in his long black coat, looking the part of the greatly gifted one, and announced he was going to the pharmacy. For me. To get me my prescription.

While I emptied my bladder I had a terrible thought. I hurried back to the bedroom and went straight for my purse. My last diamond ring was gone.

He had not left yet. I stood on the stairs, feverish, heavier then ever in my flesh. I demanded it back. Immediately. He handed it over. Strange that I should feel inhibited to ask for what was mine because I felt unattractive in my dressing gown.

We had a fight. Sam got upset and blamed his mother for screaming so loud.

The neighbours would hear. That was all Gael was concerned about.

There were two new friends in my life. The radio and the television. At my parents' house I had never had a television and we only bought one when Sam turned three.

Now I saw the same faces every day and grew familiar with them. It made me feel less alone.

I had a lot less work abroad because I lacked the energy for large solo works. All my energy was spent on surviving and so I had more empty hours to fill. I was aching for something to happen and complaining about it. To him. Get a life, he said.

I listened to a woman on the radio telling a man with a polished voice that she had her first orgasm at the age of about forty. Their children had been born out of a quick hump or a drunken coupling. The sun was hitting the windows and I could see the sea's sparkling indifference to it all. How many children? Four, five, seven? I mixed the grated parmesan and gruyère and imagined the awkward fumbling. Lights off, nightie on, here, feel this yoke, hard as a bottleneck, the seed foaming, randy hissing, the name of the next child vaguely in her head, another Sinead maybe, while she lies there wet and dizzy, damp from his outburst of passion, she wants to sleep. But he keeps her awake because he is puking in the sink.

I poured out whitish liquid from a jar into a dish, and then held the empty jar up for a long time thinking abstractedly about my man's passionate lovemaking. Wondering if Vermeer's milkmaid thought of the same thing while pouring the milk out of that earthenware jar.

The presenter moved to the subject of socks. Ladies never pick up the socks that are lying around. And they hide their men's shoes till they start to do it themselves.

While slicing the pears and washing the watercress I listened to commentary on the national tractor race. An annual event for farmers. An important event since everybody seemed to have a farm in the family. I opened the kitchen door to the flood of light and heard the roar of tractor engines. My husband knew how to ride a tractor. He showed me how when we went to visit his family on a farm.

We took Sam and his Granny to meet them in the countryside. The trees, the river and the fields were shining green.

Big dogs greeted us and an uncle came out of the small building in a torn sweater and baggy trousers. He had a flat and friendly face and helped us out of the car into the mud. We stood in our wellies and waited to be invited indoors. A boy came out carrying a trombone; he'd heard I was a musician and wanted to show it to me. Then a girl came out with a trumpet followed by a whole brass band of children. Eight of them, a wind section of eight beaming with joy over the new fiddler in the family. Why were we all outside? They shrugged and laughed and blushed until we had to go inside because it started to rain.

The house consisted of one living room, one bathroom and one bedroom. The air was so thick that I felt short of breath. Sam complained that his hands were dirty and I took him to the bathroom to clean and dry them with a grubby towel. Granny sat on a greasy chair in her best Sunday clothes and read the newspaper, while the rest of us sat around the table listening to some amusing family history.

I didn't know what he was doing there, but I could see him very clearly. My father was standing in the corner of the room, shaking with laughter, ponting at a crucifix that hung on the wall.

I wanted him to go away, and sat with my head down and my nose in my sweater to avoid the stench. From that position I discovered the origin of the foul smell. A big ferret lay asleep under the table. I lifted my head up again, only to see my father looking straight at me, still smiling. I felt lost, but since my father's ghost seemed to find it all rather amusing I thought I might as well relax.

While they fried bacon and eggs and spread out newspapers on the table, I fled outdoors with Sam.

My painter husband was wearing a cap and holding a shotgun in his hand. He walked me to the edge of the field and started shooting, hitting his targets quite well. Sam was proud of him and I felt impressed, with the kind of stupefying surge of admiration you feel when you want somebody and you know he is a total idiot, so you concentrate on his physical achievements, like the way he throws a ball in a net or kicks it.

Of course there was more to Gael.

After the meal we went for a walk with Uncle and his youngest five-year-old daughter down the old train tracks. Sam and I washed our greasy paws in a stream and walked on. Until we were told to wait because the little girl had tripped and was lying on the ground. Come on now, her father said, get up. You know Our Lord fell and got up again three times. We stood and heard a rustling of leaves and heard the little girl say that she did not want to get up, because she did not want to fall three times.

Back home I stood at the window and knew that I was weak. The rain made me see sunshine in another country and made me close my eyes in order to travel there, close my ears to hear the life being lived and my nose to remember the smells that my body wanted to breathe. Further away I knew were the voices, the voices of my friends, and, even further, the voices of my parents. My voice was loud in my head, full of questions. I wanted to hit him with them until I could draw blood and dip my fingers in it. If only I could feel it flow, or at least hear the pulse. But all I heard was the bland knock of a battered bird's beak in my own body quietening to a drone. Then mute. Silence.

That silence had come with the rain, the wind, death, with the quiet people here, still living off the earth.

19

Here are the seals, dressed in sober coats. Modest enough to keep their occupation out of sight. It's underneath the surface they feed and fuck. He can walk along the sea and talk to them every day of his life, for this is his country. These here, with their long whiskers and innocence bulging from their eyes, are the Protestants of this country. Not like the watered down ones from her Nordic place. Now it is his turn to paint them, the brothers and their Lutheran lookalikes. They have a clear bark when they come to the surface of their sombre world. These creatures have been here for centuries and hold the fish of wisdom in their finned hands. And when they use their strong teeth on the pink flesh he sees that the fish are women. Wise enough to let themselves be shredded to edible pieces after they have served in life and turned from white to a bloody pink.

His woman was alive and would never have let him draw them as they are. Natural, well-dressed, charmingly behaved killers. They have their battle with the waves, the dominant waves that believe they were traitors, stole the fish and took the water to leave behind a hungry land for the other creatures.

The waves have withdrawn to leave them wet and salty and now he rubs the small stone heads and tastes the salt on his fingers while waiting for the brothers to come up. They only fold their hands over their food, never in prayer. She was a Protestant, she wanted rules and bars for his prison; strong steel with very little space in between them. He could swim now and escape because the sea was here. She was a Beguine *from Bruges, a woman who knew no sins and wore her vanity around her neck in the shape of a fine lace collar. Look at her now, dressing down to the soberness of her brother, having lost all her silly ornaments to be with him, her master. Lives in the bare Kirk of life with her offspring. Muscles her thighs and arms carrying the bags of bargains up, up, up the hill. Leaves her shoulders hard and painful, so her fiddle stays in the cupboard. It sings its own quiet tune. It moans with her complaints whenever she takes it out. He can hear the solemn verses of human suffering right through her playing, those straight notes, no vibrato at all in Bach's* Partita*. She wants him to hear it. He hears nothing but the bark of her brothers in the merciless, indifferent, monotonous rhythm of the sea.*

She has taken the devil's dog for company. Already no one understands their mutual exchange. It is a language that deafens his ears for he knows it is about him they talk. Black fur on their tongues, luxurious hatred, sharpened teeth waiting for his bones to be bared. He treats them as his pets, now that he is a master, and tells her about his people who suffered a hundred and a thousand times more than she does of hunger and cold feet. That seems to shut her up. Sitting on a bench at the seafront he sees her with her black pup at her feet, tail wagging and all, talking out loud to her folks across the sea, shamelessly shaking with self-pitying tears.

And then there is that casually dressed islander, a gentleman with a pension, who comes up to her and points his finger at her dirty dog. She stands, straight and sober, a Nordic Minerva, ready to give a just answer. Just go, he says to her, go back to your own country, wherever you come from, go. I will, she says, but what about the dog? He's Irish.

But they want her to stay and stabilize their existence, he and the seals his brothers.

He is still mad about Minerva, that gagged goddess who lives with him.

20

Antonio had arrived at the presidential suite of the best hotel in Dublin. My husband's tricks-of-the-trade Merlin who was going to make him millions.

The correct thing to do was to go out to dinner with him. I knocked on a couple of unpacked boxes to check if they might hold what I wanted to wear. I found it. A dated outfit that looked neither cool nor at all New York. Sam howled with laughter when I tried it on and shouted 'geek' at me. I had no idea what he meant by imitating a seagull like that. So I went for jeans and a torn designer black shirt. I needed to get my dress sense back, my husband said, could I not buy something up to his standards? Once more there was a sexual flash of anger that made me rip off my clothes and pull at his to get him naked as well. And ready to be consumed.

The idea was that he was going to paint a series of religious paintings. Saints or goddesses, with their favourite animals.

While we were being fed one Michelin star after the other,

Antonio discussed the deal with my painter husband. I swallowed everything with a pinch of herbs and salt and pepper – and wine of course – and didn't take notice of the subjects that were being discussed, apart from the financial side that sounded less obscure and lacked pretence. Money was money, and I would be more then happy to see it on the table in front of me.

Antonio was a classical music lover and knew everybody in that world in New York. A tough business to make money in, huh? He had heard my recordings and was impressed. But it was so hard. He knew Yitzhak and Shlomo, of course. I should know the things he could tell me. He waved his manicured hands about to emphasize the importance of his anecdotes. A diamond flashed on his little finger.

My husband smiled over his glass of Sauternes, and I nodded in agreement as to how terrible my state as a musician was. Was I letting my music slip away to be replaced by an addiction to the deep ache of anger? I squeezed my crotch underneath the impeccable white tablecloth.

Antonio seemed happy enough with our dual performance playing talented but penniless people who crawl their way through life always on the lookout for a coin. So there it was, a fat cheque, enough to survive on for a year, and my husband's firm promise to deliver the series at the end of that period.

We kissed our old pal Antonio and flew home on our newly grown wings.

Time to meet the friends and fellow artists over homemade dishes, with the doors open to the deck to let the smoke escape. These were the smokers and drinkers of the town, who also knew what they were talking and joking about whenever a politician, pop or film star, or even a society bitch, was mentioned. In between their phases of growing drunkenness I hurried up and down to the kitchen with my ridiculous porcelain filled with gourmet food. Nobody made any move to give me a hand except to uncork the next bottle. As I had no idea who or what they were talking about, I sat and ate, and ate more. My shape was slowly changing and soon I would be able to join the floating jellyfish down at the pier.

They had seen my name in the paper and they groaned that it was good; they liked my food. They stayed on until they sounded like talking amoebas. The dog was under the table, lying on her back, her belly bloated from badly digested leftovers. The cats were on top of her, and Sam was on the sofa, snoring. My friends were asleep. I was awake with the wife of an artist sitting on my lap, wailing that she loved me and was never ever going to leave me. Never ever going back to that swine. She pointed at my dog, but meant her husband.

A beard came and sat next to me, breathing spirits in my face. So it was the fiddle I played, he tapped me lightly on my one free knee, the desperate woman still hanging on to the other. Yes, you people are very talented, what with the languages and the food and all that. I looked around for the rest of the talented people before I understood what he meant. Jews, he muttered. Not a lot of those over here. Some of us, I said with heavy emphasis on the 'us', have just as little going for them as some of you lot here. Now it was my turn to pat him lightly on the balding head. I could see the morning coming in over the sea and with it a mystical light that captured me again and again every morning.

They stumbled out and thanked me, but said they could not invite me to their homes, they could never cook that way.

So nobody invited us back and that was that. They came to our table and I didn't manage to mellow them through their stomachs and turn them into my friends. They didn't allow that sort of intimacy. Somebody who visited a psychiatrist was spoken about in hushed sentences. I learned the telephone routine; when somebody asked you how you were and your leg was falling off, you were supposed to say you were fine, fine, and if you were a bore and mentioned the leg you were told that you had nothing to complain about what with the weather being so dry and sunny these last few days. I went to my room and painted everything that I wanted to say. Maybe it was good. Maybe the absence of the warm embrace of friendship makes people productive.

Meanwhile I was taking my fiddle to various green places and getting heard in castles and towns where they served steak and chips at the local Inn. Rehearsals took place in backrooms, and sometimes an odd dog would run up to the stage and bark at me in what I hoped was approval.

I got to know my fellow musicians during rehearsals and road trips. They looked at their scores through a thick mist of longing. After the concerts the drunken dreams rolled off their tongues; they all wanted to leave for the Continent, where the music was.

Here is a lovely, folksy twiddle-dee-dee for you. Listen well. And when it gets sad it comes from far away. It sailed out with the sorrow of these poor people and came back to stay.

Although he considered anniversaries and celebrations to be bourgeois, Gael did like handing out gifts. With the back-up of Antonio's promises he came home with gold and precious stones for me. Throwing them in my lap with contempt, but content with himself to be able to give in to my silly weaknesses. After all they were an investment, and he could always take them from me and sell them. That thought seemed to cheer him up. This time he promised he would ask me first. What he said cheered me up. Not that I believed him. I wanted to be cheered up. I just missed that euphoric feeling of having a future.

He was working on some striking pieces that he allowed me to see. They made me feel humble. Seals swimming around in a flooded ruin that had sunk into the sea and looked like a church. Holding salmon out to a god with a faded-out face they seemed to worship. The lines were strong enough to avoid seeming kitsch or baroque. I was there entering his realm, knelt at the altar to worship his talent. This I had learned back home. Talent was something you used to make the world yours and heal your wounds. Were they wrong back then? My parents? I was inflicting wounds on myself to produce inspiration. But my talent did not heal them. Neither did my husband's talent heal me. My father picking at the shards of his life. I held on to his opinions, to his scars.

Gael joined me in my walks with the dog on condition that we would only discuss the things he wanted to discuss, none of my usual drone now, you hear me?

This was a country that had taken me in and showed my face in magazines and newspapers. I had my own place here and he was happy for me, but I should really get more of a life and leave the country to make a serious financial contribution to our lives.

I dreaded leaving Sam behind, and I was tired of the hard years we'd had and the loss of my parents that had left me without any family apart from my brother and his good life. I feared I might never come back. But I agreed to set out for other shores.

Christmas was coming, with friends from abroad and the turkey

I had to cook for my in-laws. Through the eyes of my friends I saw another country. Eyes that saw the light changing, the rainbows above the sea, mountains that lit up for a few minutes beside others that were veiled in clouds.

Their critical remarks were exasperating; it was like listening to myself talking in a mirror. All day long I agreed with them, all night long thoughts tortured my sleep, until I dreamt that I both stood beside the bed and was in it at the same time. And I would let myself wander through the house and walk down the moonlit path of the sea till I reached the last small island, with the lighthouse lighting my thoughts one by one in a consistent rhythm of dark and light. From there I could see them all in the house asleep. Then they seemed to have died, because I had spent too much time thinking at the lighthouse. I woke up sweating as if I had been running for a century, and went to Sam's bedroom. He was asleep with his teddy bears. The light from the lighthouse beat through his bedroom window.

There was a day when we visited my in-laws with our friends, to make them realize what they were in for during the Christmas dinner. Not being proper Christians, Christmas had very little significance for us. Except for my husband and Sam who now demanded a house full of presents.

My husband was joking and jollying around town on his way to his parents. Our friends sang in the car and then turned quiet when we reached his parents' neighbourhood. Granny was at the door, agitated by the foreign invaders. She had forgotten the holy water to spray us with. We had biscuits and tea and chatted politely in the kitchen. Plastic branches and red berries hung around the holy images and the crib. I had allies now and could afford a mean giggle. Very inappropriate, but that was me.

Granny commented on how complicated our language sounded.

The Da was in his decorated grotto, sparingly lit by electric candles on the plastic Christmas tree and the giant flicker of the television screen. He waved at us all, and we stood and stared at him watching a game show on TV. The gas stove leaked and the carbon monoxide made us feel slightly giddy. Soon we were cheering along to a soccer match. The old man was in his element, shouting at the black players. Straight out of their trees they came, he said, and look at them now, playing for a European country and all. That evening we drank the deep red wine my friends had brought with them from home, and their warmth reminded me of how much I was missing.

But I had my lover's, my husband's, arms to hold me and his voice to tell me not to worry. Not to worry Sammy, not to worry doggy, catty, not even you big fat spider on the wall, not to worry. Sleep.

The fowl and the deer leapt into their mouths, juices ran down their chins, my friend asked for a tune. Her little daughter, a pal of Sam, sat at the piano and I played a Christmas song. His parents had never heard me play. She'd had enough wine, my husband's mammy, to chat away forever. She turned around and said we had such a large deck out there, could I not go and stand outside and play to the wind? Surely, it was so loud she couldn't hear herself think.

In the months after my friends left, and the money was running out, I started the senseless sobbing again that had become my way of expressing grief. Grief over ignorance, theirs and mine.

I battled with my violin, and I battled to keep my house warm and its inhabitants fed.

My painter took to roaming the city and losing his belongings along the way. Me being around so much disturbed his concentration, could I please fuck off?

I fucked off to various countries and invariably came home to weeks of household manure. The gold and stones made their way back to the pawnbrokers. Sam complained that his daddy did not pay his transport or school fees and Daddy did not know where all the money had gone. I started being a screen between Gael and the world, and its mean and ugly people.

His work was not progressing fast enough and the lease of our house was up. There they were, the little people at the door with the papers. Leases lasted longer in my country and there was such a thing as protection for people who rented a house. Here they saw things slightly differently. So we moved. I packed and unpacked and still the sea was beside us.

My music started to inhabit the house, and everywhere I went I took the blinding light that shone in the windows with me. I smelled of the gorse in the garden and my skin was soft from the early salt dip I took in the sea. I started to smile again, and people came knocking at the garden door to have a look. And stayed for the food that I served.

The car died and we couldn't afford a new one, then bits of the roof fell off, and it rained on my grand piano. Great-grandmother died and there was to be a funeral: Sam's great granny Concepta, that he'd met twice in his life. He didn't want to miss school to go and put her in the ground, but he had to. The whole clan would be there.

I woke up wet and cold at five in the morning. No idea where I was. The room looked unfamiliar and my bed was soaked. I looked up and saw the water trickle down along the wall and drip right on to my pillow. My side of the bed that had turned into a thawing fridge. I woke my husband who felt the wet patch beside him and turned away from it to continue dreaming. Downstairs in the kitchen I saw the snow falling in the garden. It was early April. The house had no central heating so I shivered up and down the stairs with towels and an iron. I ironed through my husband's sleep until the sheet was dry. Then it was time to get up. Sam and his daddy hiccuped with laughter when they saw the remains of the wet snow on the wall. They went outside and told me that the snow was just above me on the roof and had trickled down the wall on to my head.

It was so cold we ended up looking like bears going to great-granny's funeral. No taxis to be had. Sam complained that he missed the car and was told by his father that we'd have a new one by next week. Now try to remember what the dead person was called. Granny Concepta, remember?

The train was late because of snow on the tracks. Hundreds of damp people had stacked themselves in the compartment we stood in. I felt strangely comforted, breathing in other people's oxygen. What did it matter? A cold house, a wet bed and an empty purse, my child's hand was warm in mine.

They glanced coldly at us over their synthetically-clad shoulders. Here he was, Granny Concepta's favourite grandson, half an hour late with that awful woman, the poor child. Half an hour of Mass over already and we were sitting in the last row. Sam and I were sitting there numbly when a painful screeching reached our frozen ears.

It's a violin, Mummy, Sam stage-whispered, and he pinched me hard. So they had rented a fiddler instead of asking me. I raised my eyebrows at my husband. Sure they would have been afraid to ask me, he said. I was so stunned by his statement that I missed out on most of the miserable violin playing. Why? I wondered. I'd have happily played a tune for them.

All the women had plastered their faces with orange-tinted make-up, and they all wore the same skin-coloured tights. Sam and I had problems understanding the speech given by Uncle Willy. He was deaf and whispered away, while Sam kept hissing at me. What was Uncle saying? Oh, just that they all love Great Granny 'Cepta so much. I kissed the top of his head. On a private impulse of love. The snow was even denser when we left the church. A cousin offered us a lift to the cemetery. As long as we didn't mind the, well, we'd notice it ourselves. He marched us over to the fish market where his car was parked.

A good thing Granny loved fish, he laughed when we sat in the back clutching our noses, we'll be sure to think of her this way. Sam was sick at the gates of the cemetery and we decided to walk to the grave.

Nobody cried. We heard the priest but louder still were the crows above our heads. Black clothes, black birds, black umbrellas. Snow white ground, white grave, white death.

There was food and free drinks in the pub down the road. Double doors that flapped back when you pushed them open and a big space behind it with tables lined up, and plastic plates and cups, sandwiches on each plastic plate wrapped in cellophane. We sat at the corner of a table, Sam and I, while his father disappeared into the crowd. Nobody talked to us for the first half-hour, then, after several pints, people approached us. My mother-in-law kept telling everybody that I was so good not drinking at all. I never drink during the day unless I'm in the South of France, I said.

Sam got nervous and wanted to leave. He felt unsafe. But this was the house Great Granny had built. He was safe, I told him. He wandered off and left me to the sisters and aunts who by now were quite drunk. Why had I married him? What was I doing here? I realized I had forgotten what kept me there.

Selfishness, I said, getting drunk on my own selfishness, that was the reason I stayed. Because there was only him and me. But I was talking to myself. They'd gone to get more drink. Some uncles came up to me with old family photographs. I took a liking to the faces in them. Why were they not around? Sam came back and wanted to go for a pee with me in the Ladies.

The ladies stood on their unsteady legs in a circle on the wet floor in the restrooms, smoking fags, gossiping. 'There you are,' one of the aunts shrieked. 'He's gorgeous all the same, isn't he?' They closed in on him, all the aunts and cousins, and Sam started to cry.

'Crying are you, laddie?' a gulp from her glass and on she went. 'Remember, your Great Granny Concepta had a photograph of you on her mantelpiece.' I winked at Sam and he retorted that all he could remember about the old woman was that he had to go outside in the cold for a pee. That just added oil to the fire, and on they went, about how the granny had always burned a candle beside his portrait, and did the laddie know why? I grabbed my child and pushed my way to the door. Because you are the godless child, I heard them shriek.

My husband drank for another two-and-a-half hours before I told him we were leaving. There was no money for a taxi. We'll get money in the city centre, I said. A friendly family member who'd only had fifteen pints offered us a lift. We took the bus and found our way to a cash machine. 'Go on,' said my husband and handed me a card. 'Get some.' But the machine refused to spit out any money. My husband started to laugh. He knew there was nothing in the account; it was just funny to see my face.

Then I hit him hard in the face in the middle of the street and his glasses were on the pavement and there were lots of people around us and Sam was crying.

We walked home in silence. I tucked Sam into his cold bed and stroked his head and said I was sorry. Then I confronted Gael, demanding to know what was with him, provoking me while I was struggling to keep us going. He looked at me coldly, and calmly asked me who I thought I was, talking to him like that.

I was the woman who answered the phone to people who called him a thief and a crook. I was the one who had inherited a valuable painting from her parents. He was the one who had taken it and sold it without asking her. I was the one who refused to believe what people said about him. I was the one he called ten times a day, no matter what part of the world I was in, while I was never allowed to call him, in case he was concentrating and not to be disturbed. I was his maid, scrubbing, cooking, ironing the shirts he insisted on wearing. I was the one. The one who admired his work. He was the one who had promised her a future with a big house and cars and horses running alongside, all for them, her and her son. *His* son. He was the husband who could lay waste, lose and destroy, he was the creator, the genius, the master of the perfect lie. And I was the woman who had just discovered that you could hate the person you love. All this I wanted to say but could not.

Antonio was happy with the bits and pieces he received and sent a final cheque to encourage him to finish the work. Word went around the art world that the work was going to do very well. Even if it was tough now and we said harsh things to each other, soon we would be able to live properly.

21

Now he is free to paint, because the gods have given him the light. They have shown him the path to the moon. They have conquered the sun and clouded its burning. They have presented him with the ultimate vision. Soon he will present them with his completion. The sea is sound and he is so sane in every belief he enters on every holy ground he treads. They have embraced him, the gods, and have led him to their silence, their divine ignorance. He wades from one large pocket of emptiness towards the next one of nothingness, to be cleansed of his past and look at his hands, always ready for work. Did he not buy them a castle, did he not build them a city, did he not create a cheerful crowd in all his future dreams? They sat on the towers of books and all of them had it written. From those towers they could see it so clearly, they could read the names of the ones who wrote the future. He shared this with them and gathered them to him in his robes, his wife and child. Fatimah has her eye on the world and their son has his eye on him. He bedded Fatimah and she became one of his wives before the prophet. His son is the prophet of his people. Small people who walk the earth without casting their shadow. His son and his hope, he will ride it soon and not feel the hard ground again. Ever.

He can already walk above the ground, his feet bare like a lucky beggar who knows he does not need any shoes to be with them: the fearless gods.

He has been allowed to open the windows of the great mosque and lead the people in to watch his life unfold. In his image he paints in blasphemous pleasure the forbidden creatures and himself with them, tailed and winged, furred and finned.

Cormorants winged and veiled, flying chadors, beaks closed on secrets, her sisters sit on a rock. She joins them every day to contemplate his downfall and spreads the width of her wings to block out the sea and show him the power of feathered unbending black. Their claws hold on to greater things than his ephemeral images of sea and light, they hold on to slippery stones carved out in ancient times. They are creatures born out of the water who carefully watch the ones that come from the land.

These took to veils white and black and narrowed down their lives. For a few bearable centuries they were close: Mohammed's daughters and the brides of Jesus Christ. The laws were those of the brutally religious robed males, and they took to their rocks and confined the sinless sisters to their huts. Sisters who stole the word and shed their wrappings to bare themselves in another world later, much later.

But the cormorants remained the same and never spoke. Like his Fatimah, who carries his secret and keeps it from him with the sea.

Still he hits the shore and is pulled back again by a current that prevents him from ever reaching the inner painting.

22

The dog and my husband were snoring. I was awake and feeling sick.

The six-month lease was up and the movers had come to take our things. On a Sunday they came in a big old truck. The driver wore a black patch over his eye and looked like a pirate. We hadn't managed to find a new place yet and were camped on the floor in the house of a friend, the mother of Sam's best pal.

With what we had left I suggested leaving the country and finding a cheap and pleasant place in the south of France. Sam had nearly finished his primary school and had done well. Sam and his father loved this country and were willing to sleep on its streets if necessary. But Ireland held no future for us, I thought; it was too expensive to lead a civilized life in. After ten days of camping and suffering stomach pains, however, my husband came and shook a new lease under my nose.

This one was not beside the sea. I sat on the floor and did

nothing. Concerts were announced in the paper with my name and photograph on the posters.

He kept saying he couldn't finish it without the sea.

When I went with him to look at the paintings, they looked finished to me. I gave him my advance payments for the concerts, a few months' rent, which left me without the wherewithal to buy a meal.

We'd had our usual fight before I left; I'd entered the forbidden zone of his studio. I needed the mobile phone with me on tour. Calling from a hotel room was out of the question. It was lost in the piles of rubbish on the studio floor. I went there at night to look for it, but he woke and dragged me out, leaving me covered in bruises.

The next day he said he was sorry and that he would come and see me at my hotel. He did, and we made love. We ate sandwiches, then made love again, and felt lost to ourselves. We talked about people and politics until it was time for him to take the train back home. It was strange to hide from my colleagues like that. I hid my bruised arms as I hid my hunger. A woman can always be on a diet. The art of excuses had to be perfected. Ah no, I liked walking back from the concert hall, no need for me to share a taxi. Soon the biscuits at the interval became more important to me than my solos.

They took his paintings, Antonio and his assistants, and declared them finished. He wanted them back and screamed at them until they let go and handed them over again.

I stood in a public phone box and listened to the hysterical optimism in his voice. Everything had gone really well with Antonio, he just wanted to make a few changes to the work and then, then we were going to be rich. I ran out of credit.

Sam was staying with his friend, and when I rang him a few days later his father answered the phone. He had left our house because the rent couldn't be paid. Had I not given him enough? Ah no, he needed that for something else. Not to worry now, our things were safely packed and stored away. My scores, my paintings, my piano in storage? Yes, and in a few months time the money would be here for his finished work and we would buy a house and get our things back. I wanted to believe him.

The tights were going to cost me too much. They were the price of my fare. My fare they would pay in a month's time. Nobody could tell that there were holes in my tights underneath the dress.

We were rehearsing in a morgue: it was free rehearsal space. My hands were cold, but I still had gloves. Hang on to those, new ones are out of the question. Don't lose anything. Check. Check again. A sandwich, toothpaste. For the day. This day is cold. What is it I am doing?

Maybe I can get a warm bite tomorrow before the concert, remember what you have to play. Sam and his daddy are far away. In which house? It changes every month. Sam has his books and studies in front of other people's TVs; he gets up out of other people's beds early in the morning to go to school. Sam, who told me that his daddy had taught him how to travel without a ticket. Why could I not have a million tentacles and juggle with bills and payments? The chores continued. Cook, play, clean, pay, wash and check, play again and get paid. Where was he living, what was he telling his classmates, his teachers? I was a failure, my son had lost his home. He had put his bed and his medals for horse-riding into storage, along with everything else. My son had parents who could not get them back. They were all he had.

What is it I am playing? Marin Marais.

Listen, listen to this and how I remember encountering this music for the first time.

I was leaning against the wall, long, red boots touching my thighs under a short skirt, small flowers in my hair that hung over an embroidered jacket. The teacher of baroque music had a Breughel face, his hair flowing, black. He had looked at her often in the narrow hallways of the academy, with lust and fear because she was sixteen and he was thirty. They had never said a word to each other.

I stood leaning outside his room, listening to him play. It was a less polished sound than I had been taught. Closer to the open air, the shriek of a bird of prey, the passion of the gypsy for freedom. Ringing sounds, come closer to the door they said, soaring sensuality pulling through my body, his body handling the bow. My hand on the door handle now, I wanted to know. I stayed with him for two hours, and never spoke to him again after that. Just gazed at his photograph on the record sleeve and listened to him playing for me only, succumbing to the romance I had written for myself.

And ten years later I buy the score and it becomes my music, and he leans against the pillar in a church to listen to me, and again we don't say a word to each other. I play it for him now, naked for him. Entirely naked.

My breath accompanied me in little puffs of cloud as I walked to the bus stop. Was I not coming for a drink, some musicians asked me? I was tired, I said, though that wasn't true. It had been cold on the path to the moon in our first house, and yet I missed it. Now I was frozen with the wind's harsh complaints close to my ears.

A few people came out of the woodwork offering their friendship.

A house for a period of eight or nine months. Again there were telephone calls, angry voices telling me about my husband's debts. My gallery wanted new work. I was wanted to play on the continent. But there were plane and boat fares to be paid in advance. I couldn't go. Sam needed me. My husband needed me. I had to choose between food or washing powder at the supermarket. We were going to be rich soon.

Meanwhile he walked the streets, secretly selling valuable belongings of mine, including the first painting I had made for him.

He took the dog for a long walk, so long I never saw it again.

Someone called, asking me to play a Bach concert. He said he was sending a journalist over to interview me. To this empty house? I persuaded the music shop to rent me a piano by showing them my contract for the concert.

My husband was whispering on the phone early in the morning.

Just clear away some furniture, make space for the piano, it is coming. I visualize a piano and students in the borrowed house that is mine for a while. I gather flowers from the garden and decorate the mantelpiece for the photograph in the newspaper. I wait for the doorbell. All day rehearsing Bach.

They said that she looked like the Klimt painting of the young woman in evening dress showing the dark cherry nipple of one breast. Her hair piled on top of her head, her decadent smile. The sophisticated rings on her hands. The simple white dress she chose for the concert. Bach being played in the city of music. Where the listeners were solemn in their conservative love of the composer and forgot about him throwing his wig in fury at his pupils or siring an army of illegitimate children in his spare time. She is his pupil still. She is taught by the maestro who had what Bach wanted, what Bach meant, passed on to him from generation through generation. The maestro is conducting tonight in the old concert hall where nothing ever changes. Inside that building there have been no wars or even peace negotiations. There has only ever been music.

She walks between the two young men, holding their arms to help keep her balance on impossibly high heels. As soon as the hall is reached she brushes them off softly: she would like to be alone now. Alone in her seat when the lights go out and the music flares up. But now she suddenly sees herself sitting there, she has the name of the woman in the painting, the assimilated one who shows her flesh and can afford to. The music comes to her with all its clarity. She admires the coldness of the precision but she is still waiting when it is all over, waiting for the song.

And there are her suitors again at the bottom of the velvet-covered stairs. They are going to greet the maestro.

He embraces her and invites her for the *souper* afterwards, after the signing of autographs and nodding to admirers. She waits for him and is distracted by his professional small talk.

'Yes, yes,' he totally agrees with the tall gentleman who shakes his hand, 'Jews should not play Bach, anything else, yes, absolutely, but not Bach.' He sees her looking at him and he winks. When the crowds are gone he grabs her arm and whispers in her ear that this man is a formidable sponsor. So you don't agree? 'Well,' he touches her cheek, 'I think we should discuss that over supper.' She asks her suitors to go home and to please get her violin.

Again she walks the city between them. Her violin is on her back on the way to the famous restaurant where the maestro is having supper with some friends. Already she is known for her talent amongst these people. She climbs on to the table before they have noticed her and stands between the porcelain holding her violin, lifting her arm so that her dress opens up too much and shows the cherry-red of her nipple. She plays the Partita. 'Never heard it played so well,' says one of the biggest music agents in the world before he clears his plate. The maestro is not smiling. She will never play in this city again.

I phoned the shop to inquire about the piano. The man on the phone sounded surprised. My husband had been there yesterday to get the deposit back. I asked him about it that night. 'You know what your problem is?' – he did not look me in the eye – 'You are far too focused on me. You really should get out more.'

I told him I would get out a good deal more. That as a matter of fact I was getting out for good the next morning.

23

The man is the monk is the master. His desires are purified. He has cast her off like an old snakeskin and is keeping that skin in a cupboard. A parchment memory with fading folds and flakes written all over it. To remember her, he reads it with his hands like a blind man reads Braille. He recognizes her, but he does not recognize the animal that the skin belonged to.

He sleeps with his paintings in rooms that he finds around the city. He does not beg for food or money. A monk gets what he deserves. People worship him, bring him goods, offer him blankets and a coat. Want to share his infinite wisdom. Like what the colours stand for and why they have to breathe it every day, the same monotonous green. And he tells them it is not monotonous, it is the eternal green. It is not an island, it is a planet drifting on a coloured sea of time. Surrounded by animals that do not share their stupid presumptions about life. He shows them how the state of being early or late is a laughing matter, for who is to say. Build your own time, paint your own hours, live the longest minute if that is your wish. Swim the waters with the seals and the fish, dance to the bird tunes, bark with the dogs if you must. Even in Ireland these things are possible. Soon he will become the Irish Guru and his paintings will become holy. Sometimes he walks with his son to show him the way of his world. And when he is gone, he sits again in time. Time was his master and forced him to spoil his divine work. Now he has spoken with Buddha and has become the master of time. He is not with his herd anymore. He has strayed into a new eternity where nothing can touch him. Feelings were never his forte, it was the thought that brought him all this, these paintings. He still hears the names. His son and his son's mother are present when he says the names. And Antonio. Antonio is a presence that carries a promise. To pay for the goddesses that he painted. They did not believe in him, they became one huge dismissive creature surrounded by their reality. He had Maria, Laxmi, the Banshee and Fatimah. But there is no need for them now. A future. He can now build on his future forever. He feeds his body enough to become light, so light that he can feel himself floating slightly above the ground. Other bodies had dragged him down in the past. No need for those anymore.

The flesh does not partake of time. He moves his body along in the city and meets meditating monks like himself, creations of Buddha. Not that he speaks to them. Language is for the poor of mind. Everything is written and found within silence. Silence was the music she could never produce.

24

We had two rooms, Sam and I. Sometimes heated up by a fire, mostly chilly. The damp made my fingers curl in to a comic cramp. Sam laughed when he saw me unfold my hands in the morning. His laughing cheered me up. As long as he was in the rooms, and I tried to make his life enjoyable , those arthritic hands were bearable. The conductors did not even smile when I said I needed more time to warm up. My sound was croaky at the beginning of rehearsals. I didn't have enough strength left in me to join an orchestra. Whenever I tried I heard a surprised manager on the phone who wondered why I, a soloist, would want to join an orchestra. In any event I couldn't leave the country because I had to look after Sam. Sam needed his food and books and money to spend on ridiculous 'cool' things with his teenage friends. My friends found it harder to reach me. I had no phone or computer.

But I had my two cats to talk to and stroke their warm bellies if they needed affection. I needed none. No men's hands or lips. The threat was too great. Behind every gentle gesture I saw the gaping void, the burning venom of love.

I met women who avoided the subject of men. I, too, felt that there was nothing I wanted to share with the male species. Not even an orgasm.

We had our knock on the door every evening, Sam and I. It was his father, standing on the steps in front of the house, shivering slightly. Sam would come out with an umbrella and some coins and spend some time going over his schoolwork sitting on the stairs. My landlady had strong objections to my husband coming into the house. At first she had quite liked his entertaining stories and she had let him in, during my absences, out of the rain or the cold, sure the poor fellow couldn't be that bad. But then she claimed that things went missing in her quarters and she wouldn't have him around any more. I couldn't believe it was him. It was more the stories that circulated about him and must have reached her eager ears. Stealing from other people's houses would have been too much of an effort for my husband. He couldn't have dealt with the fear. Most of the time we never knew where he lived or slept. He seemed to be clean enough when occasionally we had sex. He was no longer a man but a zombie, who flirted with religions and sometimes remembered the functions of his body. Sam cheerfully denied there was anything wrong with him. I was the mad one who had walked out on his adored father. He didn't like me for it. But he did like my kisses and my presents and the fact that I was a real parent, one that you could annoy and curse and kick.

I had no access to my belongings so our rooms had bare walls and scanty furniture, except for two paintings – one belonging to my husband that he had entitled 'The Wrong', and, ironically, one by my father that he had named 'The Right'. I was cradled between the two each night, dreaming of some kind of equilibrium. Even in my dreams there were problems to be solved and obstacles to be considered, but the moment I awoke and stumbled to the stove to cook Sam's breakfast my priorities changed. Sam left very early with his bag on his back and faint circles under his eyes. They would disappear during the day, but then the finest of wrinkles on his brow would have replaced them by the evening. I would stare at my husband's painting and feel bloodless, limp, unable to do anything to make it change. All I could do was to struggle on my violin and try to make small drawings for children's books that made me a little money.

My bed was a mattress on the floor. I could touch the hard planks if I reached out. They felt like some kind of truth, as if there was really nothing more to truth than air and hard surface and my anxious breathing in between. I read Nietzsche and put the book in a corner on the floor with the others. We had no shelves for them.

Hard to explain to my friends or my brother abroad that I sometimes ran out of money that enabled me to keep my arse clean. The big needs were not provided for at all. Dentist and doctors had to be avoided at all costs. In the evening we would study Sam's homework and lie in bed watching the tiny screen of our TV.

Sometimes I was my old self and would go into a clothes shop dressed in the remains of my designer clothes. I could still act out the woman who knew all about fashion and could afford it. I was just a stingy eccentric who wore her expensive clothes into shreds before acquiring new ones. Or the sentimental one who was so attached to her garments that she found it impossible to be separated from them and left them to rot. I fed the dream for a few hours and felt stupidly elevated and good.

In my bed I folded my arms under my head and lay on my back focusing on the bare spot in between the two paintings. It grew dark and in that dark it lit up: the writing on the wall said Santorini.

Black beaches and straight sea. The suspicion of sharks circling the depths of the swimming waters. A Greek island on which they had sharpened their pencils every day of their holiday. Finding subjects to draw was what they discussed in the morning, what silenced them during the afternoon when they rode donkeys to go down and dip their brushes in the sea and swim to wash the efforts of colouring away. The sun would go down on them while they rested on a pier built in a small sandy bay. Once they saw a boat with faded colours. It came drifting in from its own saga, carrying a horse, a goat, a cow, a sheep and a couple of toothless old gods who held up a lobster to them.

They fixed a fire of twigs and roasted the crayfish for themselves. They laughed so much when they watched them eat showing their naked gums to the full. Happy, happy they clapped their hands while they walked away and left them with the helpless claws.

They slept in the sand, snakes nearby, heard but never seen in the low bushes. Morning came to reveal a calm, blue basin of salty sea. Never been crossed by the likes of a boat. Or so it seemed. They had to reproduce it, paint what they had seen. They did and she forgot about her music for weeks. His body, hers, was all there was to that warm vacation. Until they made it to a terrace of a café built high above the sea, where they sat alone in the evening. To listen to Brahms suddenly sounding through bad speakers. On Santorini, island of burnt-out volcanoes, the volcano within her had burst. He held her hand because she cried as she watched the fine line of notes disappear over the water, but he had no idea why.

25

I went to a pub and asked for a job. Playing a few tunes, enough material to tell the public about my life in Ireland in between the music. I had to be a bit of a glamorous bird, standing there with my stories, a tittering phoenix rising from her self-induced ashes.

Sam went to England at the end of his summer holidays. Apparently his daddy had found a way to make money, and I thought it would be okay for him to spend some time with his father.

I went through my routine for the tourists – you lot – and waited for his return to our rooms, feeling more and more as though I was turning into a ghost.

The knock on the door at four in the morning. They must be back, I thought.

It was him, without our child. A suffocating sense of panic. Where was my child?

Sit down, woman, he said, just sit down. He had sold his

paintings, he said, for a lot of money. Took Sam to that boarding school with the horses that he always wanted to go to. Paid for the remaining school years, gave the child money. They had gone to the Races and had a few bets, yes, and the boy had got drunk with him. First time. Had a tattoo put on his bum, right near the inside of a cheek. A Star of David, you know, so he can shite on it when he has the runs. Went to the races the next day. Lost the rest of his money. As usual. He laughed about something. I had never known where it went. The money. On betting. Spent talent, blown away. There was surely somewhere he couldn't find me. Or, like my father, did I need to suffer in order to achieve? Mistress Pain I had called love.

If I murdered him I could turn him into an angel, maybe. If I killed myself would I become one?

Quite coldly I put the question to him. It all seemed logical to him. As a Jewess, my soul would simply travel to another body. Imagine, you can be like all of those great violonists: Jasha Haifetz, Ida Haendel, Izak Perlman, Shlomo Mintz. That's what you wanted, hey? You could have been as good as them, that's what you think, hey? Well here's your second chance, sweetie, take the jump. I started to kick him and he ran.

26

He feels he is becoming the wisest of men. A rebel. Sam has joined him in his search for the ultimate secret. How to start all over again, now that he has wasted his paintings on fools and buffoons who threw money at him. They have crossed waters and Sam has gone with the horses. He has brought him to a blacksmith. But first of all he laid down his head on the anvil. Begged the smith to reshape it with the glowing heat of his brain. Hammer on its turmoil until chaos has a shape at last.

Sam is waiting at the stables. His hand on the soft nostrils of the horses until the blacksmith comes and brings him over to the anvil. Sits and puts his feet in his pardoned lap. Tender skinned hooves to be gently shoed for every type of ground. You little Jew man, you never know which way you will have to go. Just joking, all that is gone now, we know that much out here. You are all rich now, what with your own country and all that. And horses to ride. It used to be donkeys for you lot. Not any more. Not any more. And your father who comes from our church, now look at him. A rebel. His loud laughter echoed the thunder of the galloping herds. Nothing is evil in nature, neither his innocent laugh nor their senseless speed. Only his father. His father will not knock at the door anymore or read from the books. He will read from them himself and make the commentaries come to life. There are shelves in his room filled with games from the Torah and the Kabbalah. Don't smash the puzzle, sort it out. Even if it takes him a lifetime. What he feels he must use for a higher purpose. Like painting.

He is not to miss the mother who raised him. Look, there she is. You can see her from the window of your new room. A dapple-grey creature will talk to you. And make you forget, running against your memory. Racing, if necessary. This is what you always wanted, to compete with time on horseback. To rest with your favourite books in your own room. To walk with classmates and be equal. Your father is good.

We had your bum branded with the symbol of your mother's race. We shared some firewater. Enough to bottle our last sane thoughts up and keep them for posterity. He must teach him the significance of the universe now that he wears the rebbe's robe. The beard that hides the smile. The side locks that he hides when he pays for his son's exquisite boarding school. It feels right to be this way. Look at the strong animals. So much freedom, Sam. Here is his chance to live. Ignore humanity. He painted his life. He did it. It brought him here, the spirit of his work. Not music. His mother will not come at bedtime. If Sam needs it he will bring him her violin in its pretty coffin. If Sam needs something, anything, he will be what he needs. The Messiah.

27

Sam was happy over there. I spoke to him on the phone and I heard grass and clouds in his voice.

Tell me what to do, people. Murder or suicide? I know you're all bastards; you haven't been listening. Tomorrow he will come back, my husband the painter.

You tell me, Loth. Yes, I recognized you immediately. My first husband, he's sitting right there, folks. He hasn't lost his hair or his looks at all. Still the elegant man. Seems to have materialized all the way from France. The husband who pushed my talents and spoiled my tastes. We have to have a chat in a minute. Please stay. Good to see you. Tell me, all of you, what shall I do? Thank you. A tune?

Thank you again. Goodnight.

28

She turned to stone, a pillar. A statue of salt.

God had moved to Paris a long time ago. At least Loth had had that feeling for a few decades now. Ever since she had left, so to speak. He knew he was a man of his city and shared its delirious memories of the nineteenth century when it had been dictating culture and science to the rest of the world.

By just being there she had added an extra dimension to his two-dimensional life. She had been able to pull him out of that life with her mad dancing and horrendous tastes for popular music, all the while toying with the Great Romantics on her instrument.

She still got the sound right, even in those slight tunes he had just heard her perform. Her hands had suffered. He could take her to a good doctor, the best.

Her skin was flawless now that she was up close to him. It had been the cruel light that made her look gaunt. She was skinny and her hair was dyed too harshly, but that could be remedied easily enough back home. He still felt attracted to her. He had been listening to her speak for hours. She was quiet now, waiting for him to say something. Tell her what to do, to improve her marriage maybe. They were sure to be a lot better off if one of them turned into an angel. It was bound to be bliss. He did not know where his voice came from when he added that she should come home now, back to Paris with him. He had seen enough.

She agreed without much hesitation. Sam could visit her there when he had time off boarding school. She wanted to go back to one spot. Torca Point. See the landscape once more and try to understand just once more how the son of that landscape could be evil. She would join Loth in Paris. He would leave her ticket at Dublin Airport for the following night. That should leave her time for her last sentimental journey. Again she agreed and kissed him on the cheek. It was a cold evening. He gave her his coat and took a taxi back to his hotel.

There were so many flowers that reminded him of her back at his apartment. Camelia floating in crystal pink and red skin and lips. White tulips in the bathroom, petals dropping from a fresh erect stem. Primroses, bushy and mildly wild like her, in her uncrushed hair. The big roof terrace overgrown with her fairytale stockroses.

He stood on the terrace looking at the fountain on the Place de la Concorde. Had she turned into one of those mermaids, the one staring straight at his apartment keeping her stone gaze fixed on him?

They raised their glasses to her and her beautiful taste in flowers, Loth and all her old friends. They drank to her funeral.

29

Here she is with her small case on her back, looking for dolphins to play to, without our child. Lonely without her child. Our son. Under this impeccable sky I am here again. This time I call her. She hears me and calls me by my name; how clean it sounds in the open air. 'Gael, Gael is that you?' Did she finally hear me that last time when I told her she could be all of them, just to let her soul fly out there in between the light horizon and the dark waters and pray for it to go to another musical body? I can come out of my hiding place now that I am God and just as visible as invisible. So close beside her that I can catch her breath. She touches me. Can she see me? I am not too sure. But when I talk to her she listens. Now she looks at me. The silver lightning in her eyes does not scald my nerves anymore.

I am free to show myself to her. She stands like a statue petrified by her vision of me.

Woman, let me help you this once, let me tell you what to do. Take off your clothes, dress yourself in the naked truth.

How magnificent they are: her feathered arms. I can hear the soft crackling of the fragile bones still growing into the pinkish inner nerve of her wings. You always believed in me. Now trust me once more. We are going to fall together. For good and evil. These are your rewards. Let me stroke them. Don't panic if you can't feel them, or see me. I am here. I am yours. I am God. You want to come with me. Just start your flight. There is only room between these rocks for one takeoff at a time. I am the gentleman – you can go first. Let me help you. There you go. Pity the flight is so short. Feel my hand on your back. There, there you go. Your choice: rocks or water, water or rocks. We both like to gamble. Remember?

She does not fly, she does not fall. Dissolves the cormorants, dismembers the seals, her wings spread as wide as far as foam on the eternal firmament.

She has left me behind.